GRUDGES

By

Joe Queenan & T.J. Elliott

© 2019-2023, T.J. Elliott & Joe Queenan

In Collaboration with

Off The Wall Plays

https://offthewallplays.com

This script is provided for reading purposes only. Professionals and amateurs are hereby advised that it is subject to royalty. It is fully protected under the laws of the United States of America, the British Empire, including the Dominion of Canada, and all other countries of the Copyright Union. All rights, including but not limited to professional, amateur, film, radio, and all other media (including use on the worldwide web) and the rights of translation into foreign languages are strictly reserved; and any unauthorized use of the material may subject the user to any and all applicable civil and criminal penalties. No part of this publication may be reproduced, distributed, or transmitted in any form or by any means, including photocopying, recording, or other electronic or mechanical methods, without the prior written permission of the publisher or author, except in the case of brief quotations embodied in critical reviews and certain other noncommercial uses permitted by copyright law. Although every precaution has been taken to verify the accuracy of the information contained herein, the author and publisher assume no responsibility for any errors or omissions. No liability is assumed for damages that may result from the use of information contained within. For any information about royalties or to apply for a performance license please click the following link:

https://offthewallplays.com/royalties-and-licensing-of-plays-sold-by-off-the-wall-plays/

"Reasons for anger are not eternal. People who store away grievances for years only to 'reactivate' them when it is convenient to do so are not rational. They are displaying a vice: that of holding a grudge."

Agnes Callard, The Reason to Be Angry Forever

"Anger may be defined as a desire accompanied by pain, for a conspicuous revenge for a conspicuous slight at the hands of men who have no call to slight oneself or one's friends.... It must always be attended by a certain pleasure — that which arises from the expectation of revenge. ... Again, we are angrier with our friends then with other people, since we feel that our friends ought to treat us well and not badly."

Aristotle, Rhetoric Part II, Translated by W. Rhys Roberts

4

CHARACTERS

Matthew McCarthy, a college professor, and proprietor of a small publishing house, in his late fifties

Faith Vergaretti McCarthy, his wife, retired high school teacher, slightly younger, manages the publishing house

Paul McCarthy, his older brother, an extremely successful "financial guru," in his sixties

Candelaria "Candy" Cruz, Paul's "inamorata," a political operative in her thirties

Jerry Marcus, Matt & Faith's next-door neighbor, an African-American Adonis, in his fifties

(A note on singing: songs are in the public domain, or lines are fair use. Paul offers nonsense scat or fragments of conversational trifles, such as "missed you")

(The '//' sign at the end of a line indicates that the character speaking next talks over the end of that line.)

Grudges was first produced on Zoom live streamed for an international audience by Knowledge Workings Theater LLC (Executive Producer — Marjorie Phillips Elliott) in July of 2019. Dora Endre directed assisted by Emma Denson with Gifford Elliott as technical director and Ed Altman as Narrator

The cast was as follows:

MATTHEW .... John Blaylock

FAITH .... Lynne Otis

PAUL .... James Lawson

CANDELARIA (CANDY) ..Jasmine Dorothy Haefner

JERRY ....Andre Montgomery

*(It is November 2018. Lights rise on the
charming, well-appointed Montclair,
New Jersey, cottage of Matthew
McCarthy and Faith Vergaretti, his wife
of many years. We see a backdrop of a
wall with the front door to the house,
and two rooms separated by a wall with
a swinging door. The rooms are rarely
illuminated at the same time. Stage right
is a living/dining room with two wooden
stacking chairs, a small sofa, a
"secretary" piled high with books, and a
folding table against the wall, which will
be opened during the evening. There is
also a door that leads to a powder room.
On the other wall is a sound system with
some LPs displayed, including the
Beatles' White Album. Stage left, behind
the other wall, is a kitchen with counter
and stove to the back. Matthew, late-
fifties and slightly academic in his looks,
enters from the kitchen in a rush with
Faith, in her early fifties and quite, quite
pretty, close behind.)*

MATTHEW

(progressively louder) No.
No. No. Sorry, let me
rephrase that. *No.*

FAITH

Don't be irrational.

MATTHEW

Irrational? Self-preservation
is the quintessence of
rational behavior. Ask
Freud. No, better still, ask
Custer.

FAITH

Self-preservation? A rat
escaping a sinking ship,
leaving me to face...//

MATTHEW

*(taking her arm and steering
her toward the door)* Fine, so
here's an alternative to your
surprise dinner plans: We
flee the premises, repair to
the local bistro, and put this
unfortunate incident behind
us.

FAITH

Don't be ridiculous. We can't
leave now. Paul will be here
any minute.

MATTHEW

(He escapes to the kitchen, where she follows him as he grabs a seltzer can from the refrigerator.) And if we're not here when he arrives, he'll go away, and later we'll just say that we wrote down the wrong date. An honest mistake. Like Saint Peter missing Christ's crucifixion: "Oh, I thought it was *next* Friday!" *(He tries to get by her, but she blocks him.)*

FAITH

You're going to stay and you're going to gut it out. Because you're not a coward.//

MATTHEW

(interrupting and assuming an actorly voice) "I tell you this, my friend: all men are cowards."

FAITH

(interrupting) Save your fancy quotations for your hapless, drowning-in-debt students. They should see

their hero now. Also
drowning in debt.

MATTHEW

(making imaginary note)
Add Paul's visit to my
lecture on fight-or-flight
syndrome.

FAITH

Matthew, *tesoro. (takes his
hand)* You — *we* — haven't
seen Paul in ages.

MATTHEW

So what? I follow him on
Instagram. I even tap in the
occasional "like" after
sneaking a peek at one of his
spectacular Seminole
sunsets. *(fingering some of
the volumes on the
secretary)* And I skim his
hideous books. *How to Make
Money Off the Coming
Apocalypse. Navigating the
Armageddon Yield Curve.
Frack and Ruin.*

FAITH

Stop it. Those are not Paul's
book titles. Check that:
They're not Paul's *best-
selling* book titles. *(beat)*

Come on, Matthew, we are talking about your *brother*!

MATTHEW

(pause) Abel was Cain's brother...

FAITH

You and Paul were close.

MATTHEW

Romulus and Remus were close. Like that. *(crosses fingers to indicate closeness)* Then Mrs. Remus scheduled a convivial dinner, and...

FAITH

Mary, Mother of God, stop joking. Back in New York, when things looked *really* bad, who visited you in the hospital every day? Not your other so-called friends...//

MATTHEW

(grudgingly) Yes, yes, yes. We were close. Once. And true, Paul does have certain fine qualities. But so did Pol Pot. Great around kids. *(FAITH shoves him playfully.)*

FAITH

Oh, cut it out, Matthew.

MATTHEW

(suddenly serious) You cut it out, Faith. Why did you invite him without asking me? Remember that *last* Thanksgiving dinner? Disaster. It was like the Bataan Death March. Without the fragrant basmati rice.

FAITH

I didn't invite him. I answered my phone and he told me that he was passing through New York and wanted to see us. Look, it's only dinner. And he'll be on his best behavior. No arguments. He promised.

MATTHEW

Impossible. Paul is an argument addict.

FAITH

And you're not?//

MATTHEW

(shaking his head) Yes, okay,
I argue with others. But Paul
gets into arguments when
there's nobody else in the
room.

FAITH

Matthew, he's your brother.
(embracing him) And *our* old
singing partner. And I never
get to sing anymore. It'll be
fun. He won't talk about...
their guy. Those are my
ground rules: Under this
roof, between these four
walls...

MATTHEW

Isn't it *"among"* these four
walls?

FAITH

(staring him down)
Whatever. Here, in this
house, he does not say *that*
name out loud. Ever. And in
return, we don't say the
other name. The good name.
The progressive name. *Our*
guy's name. You know.

14

MATTHEW

You mean the one he calls
the Magic Kenyan? And he
agreed to this? Impossible.
Not being able to repeat the
name of that pestilential
pustule down on
Pennsylvania Avenue every
thirty seconds will eliminate
ninety percent of his
conversation. What will that
leave us to talk about?

FAITH

Family. Baseball. The human
condition. Or *(beat)* – how
about this? -- our publishing
business. He's an author;
you're an author.

MATTHEW

He's an author in the same
way Deepak Chopra is an
author. He diligently
assembles rectangular
objects bearing a startling
resemblance to actual
books.

FAITH

Come on. Think of how
much fun it'll be when we
start to sing. Because we *are*
going to sing. We'll drink,

and we'll eat, and then we'll
sing. Come on. You always
talk about trying to be your
best self.

MATTHEW

That's aspirational. Like
taking up the hammered
dulcimer.

FAITH

*(She laughs despite herself
and embracing him again
forces him to look into her
eyes.)* At Thanksgiving, every
year, in front of the kids and
the cousins and the forty
other people you always
make me invite, we all bow
our heads and start to cry
when you recite that prayer
by Robert Louis Stevenson?
How does it go...?

MATTHEW

*(assuming actorly voice
again, returning her
embrace)* "Purge out of
every heart the lurking
grudge... Offenders, give us
the grace to accept and to
forgive offenders."

FAITH

(interrupting him) E miracolo, your prayers are answered. Today is the Day of the Great Purgation. *(She kisses him.)* Look, I sang with you two for years. I know Paul, darling. I know the wonderful Paul, the not-so-wonderful Paul, and the massively annoying, first-class jerk Paul. But he misses you. And I'm sure that at some level you miss him. You're a matched set. The magnificent McCarthy Brothers

MATTHEW

Wow. Makes us sound *iconic*.

FAITH

You were. You are. To me. *(Doorbell rings.)*

MATTHEW

Uh-oh, I have to go get something. I'll try to be back by next Easter.

FAITH

No. *(MATTHEW exits,
retreating backwards into
the kitchen.)* No! Mother of
God. *(She gathers herself and
opens the door. Paul, early
sixties and dressed very
stylishly, is standing there.
He holds a bottle of wine, but
nonetheless throws open his
arms and twirls Faith
around.)*

PAUL

Faith! *(singing in doo-wop
style)* I missed you. Missed
you, missed you, missed you.
*(He sets her down with a
flourish.)* Oh, how I missed
you!

FAITH

*(giving him a peck on the
cheek)* I am so glad you
came, Paul. I can't tell you.

PAUL

Me too, sister. *(haltingly) Yo también, hermana. (FAITH looks puzzled, while Paul retreats to the front door and speaks to someone outside.)* Come in. *(singing)* Come in, darling! *Entra en la casa de mi hermano, querida. CANDY CRUZ, thirties, Latina, and stunning, enters. They all stand for a moment in complete silence, then PAUL speaks in grand fashion.)* Faith, this is my beautiful friend, Candy Cruz. Candy, this is my wonderful, wonderful sister-in-law Faith Vergaretti McCarthy.

FAITH

Candy. *(shaking hands)* Welcome.

PAUL

We were in the city together and...//

CANDY

(speaking over him) I hope it's okay. So nice to meet you. *Encantada.* Vergaretti? *Italiana! Chic.*

PAUL

We figured a surprise would be fun.

FAITH

Oh, you were always about fun, Paul. *(beckoning)* Fun, fun, fun.

PAUL

Well, till Daddy took the T-bird away!

FAITH

But come in. Please.

PAUL

(singing again and swinging FAITH in a sort of clumsy waltz) If you're Irish, come into the parlor, there's a welcome there for you; *(improvising)* and a welcome for the Italians and the sweet Latinas too! *(FAITH pushes him off laughingly.)* Where is my baby brother?

Did he make a break for the Canadian border?

FAITH

He'll be right out.

PAUL

What's he doing? Putting the finishing touches on another one of those books that nobody reads? *(FAITH good-naturedly smacks PAUL on the arm as MATTHEW enters with a bottle of wine.)* Matty! Matty! Hey, hey, hey!

MATTHEW

What's this about books? Are you planning to read one this year? *(FAITH pinches MATTHEW'S arm from behind as PAUL and MATTHEW hug. CANDY inspects the room. PAUL gives him a bear hug. MATTHEW goes limp, disembracing quickly.)*

PAUL

I cannot believe I'm actually back in the "sanctuary." What an honor. Should we take off our shoes? Our

socks? Is there a hazmat suit
available, so that we don't
contaminate anything?

CANDY

Oh, Paul, you are wild. You
are just so wild. Isn't he
wild?

MATTHEW

Wild as the wind. Maybe
wilder.

CANDY

(to FAITH) I love all the
white. *(FAITH nods) Un
paradiso blanco.*

FAITH

It was that way when we
moved in. Someday *we'll* get
around to painting the place.

*(MATTHEW
crosses over to
CANDY. PAUL
walks over to the
record collection
and picks up the
White Album.)*

PAUL

(loudly) Was this *my* copy of
the *White Album*? Sure looks

like it. My baby brother —
always *appropriating* other
people's property! Just like
the government! *(winks at
FAITH)* Sorry. My little joke.

MATTHEW

*(looks at FAITH balefully,
then turns to shake hands
with CANDY)* Hi. I'm
Matthew.

CANDY

I'm Candy. Cruz. With a "z.'
Actually, Candelaria. My
grandmother's name.

MATTHEW

Candelaria. That's beautiful.
Wait, wasn't there a baseball
player by that name? Played
for the White Sox?

PAUL

Pirates.

CANDY

My name comes from the
Latin word "candela,"
meaning "candle." My
Mother's idea. In fact, I was
born on the feast of the
Purification of the Virgin,

the day they bless the
candles.

MATTHEW

The Purification of the
Virgin! But, hold on, isn't
purifying a virgin
redundant? *(now relenting,
worried that CANDY will
take offense)* That is, given
her family background. And
connections.

FAITH

(to MATTHEW) Idiota! The
priest blesses the candles
and the family keeps them
lit so the Blessed Mother
will protect us.

CANDY

(grabbing FAITH'S hand)
¡*Naturalmente*! Look!
Already we have *some*thing
in common! The One True
Church!

PAUL

Dios mio, si! And just like a
candle, this one lights up the
room. *(taking CANDY'S
hand)* Oh, yeah! Got the right
girl at the right time with
the right frame of mind!

CANDY

They say right-wing women are sexier. *(showing off a bit, hand on hip)*

(MATTHEW looks at FAITH, who avoids his gaze.)

MATTHEW

Sexier than right-wing men? Absolutely.

PAUL

I think of you as more right-leaning than right-wing, *querida*. Labels limit people, *no es verdad? (turning to FAITH and MATTHEW)* This one? Very complex. Libertarian, free market, conservative — that is, true conservative. *(kissing CANDY on the forehead)* Lots going on in there.

CANDY

(taps her chest) Small government. Big heart.

PAUL

Corazon. Mucho corazon.
(overemphasizing the "z") Or
is it *muy?*

FAITH

(to PAUL) Paul, politics? You
agreed.

PAUL

Hey, hey, hey. *(singing)*
Don't you worry 'bout a
thing. *(talking)* Lots of other
stuff we can talk about. *(to*
MATTHEW) I explained
today's ground rules to
Candy, the *covenant*, if you
will, and how I made this
promise to Faith that
neither of us is going to
mention certain names. As
our President says, there's
nothing more important
than keeping promises. *(to*
FAITH) See? I didn't say his
name.

MATTHEW

Our president? What you
mean "our," *Kimo Sabe?*
*(CANDY winces at the joke,
which she is too young to
understand.)*

FAITH

Isn't referring to the
President like that a divisive
political statement, Paul?
(He spreads his hands.) No
names. You promised.

PAUL

No names. But you do accept
that *he* is our President? And
that *he* rules from sea to
shining sea?

CANDY

*Viva el Presidente! Viva
(catches herself) el...
Presidente!*

MATTHEW

Or as Faith likes to call him:
*Il Duce. (FAITH smacks him
on the back and shakes her
head "No" vigorously.)*

PAUL

(Laughs) You're not
Electoral College deniers,
are you?

FAITH

We are not. Oh, my, I see
that you've brought us some
fancy *Italian* vino. Let's give
it a try. *(MATTHEW holds up
his bottle in protest, but to
no avail.)*

CANDY

Do you have any bourbon? I
like it neat and well-aged.

MATTHEW

Neat and well-aged? Just like
Paul. *(shows his bottle
again)*

PAUL

I'm going to go full-bore
liberal here and have red
wine. Matty. You need to
taste *this one. (looks at
MATTHEWS'S label, places it
on a sideboard)* I have to
admit, blue states do have
some awfully good wines.
California. *(leaving)* Oregon.
New Jersey. *(enters kitchen*

laughing at his own joke)
Corkscrew? *(FAITH follows.*
Lights dim in the living room
and rise in kitchen where
Paul takes the corkscrew and
starts to open his bottle as
FAITH gets glasses.) Did you
tell him what we talked
about?

FAITH

(whispering and motioning
for him to do the same) No! It
has to come from you, Paul.
Just find a way to work it
into the conversation. Say
that he'd be doing you a
favor. Otherwise, it's no-go.

PAUL

(dubious) Come on, Faith.
Matty is liberal. He's not
stupid.

FAITH

Just try it my way, Paul. Stick
with the plan. And with your
promise. Please.

PAUL

Faith, I always said Matty
was a very lucky man to
have you as his wife. *(pours*
wine into her glass)

FAITH

And part of that luck is
having you as his brother.
*(He toasts her with the open
bottle as lights dim on them
and come up again on the
living room.)*

CANDY

Such a lovely neighborhood.
Paul said that you have lived
here for some time.

MATTHEW

Not that long. We downsized
when we became empty-
nesters.

CANDY

Empty-nesters! Such a sad
word! Such a sad concept!
Que tristeza!

MATTHEW

Oh, we keep ourselves
amused.

CANDY

Aha! And how do you amuse
yourselves in the empty
nest? *(pokes him)* Hmm?
Hmm?

MATTHEW

(a little embarrassed) You'll
have to ask Faith about that
one. *(silence)* Now, where is
that bourbon? *(Starts to
move toward the kitchen but
CANDY puts a hand on his
arm and slides past him.)*

CANDY

I'll get it. *(Just as she is about
to go through the swinging
door, PAUL re-enters,
holding a tray with a bottle
and two glasses of red wine.
They share a kiss while
gliding by each other. The
lights switch again to reveal
the kitchen and leave the
living room in the dark. As
CANDY enters, FAITH is
holding a glass of bourbon,
which she presents to her.)*
Perfect. I hope this isn't an
imposition.

FAITH

Not at all. *(She continues
packing a tray with hors
d'oeuvres.)* In the house I
grew up in, unexpected

guests were always
expected. *(waves her hands)*

CANDY

I'd offer to help, but *la
cocina* is not my *native*
habitat.

FAITH

That's fine. Everything's
under control. *(sips her glass
of wine)* Well, so far. *(The
lights dim there and switch
to the living room, where
PAUL and MATTHEW
simultaneously, pretentiously
swirl, sniff, and sip their
glasses of wine.)*

MATTHEW

What is this? It's good.

PAUL

*(pronouncing the name
richly) Amarone. Amarone
della Valpolicella, Classico.*
Best wine in the world.

MATTHEW

Says who? *(FAITH and
CANDY enter with drinks and
hors d'oeuvres.)*

PAUL

The *cognoscenti*, Matty.

MATTHEW

Oh, right. The *cognoscenti*.
Those guys.

CANDY

He calls you Matty. That's so
sweet.

FAITH

Not *that* sweet. He does it
because it annoys him.

CANDY

And what do you call him in
return?

MATTHEW

Daddy's Big Regret? The
Bringer of Darkness?
Droopy Drawers? That was
our mother's childhood
nickname for Paul.

FAITH

Matthew!

PAUL

Still sharp, my little brother.
Could've been a contender.

MATTHEW

Contending for what?

FAITH

Moving right along, how did
you two meet?

CANDY

We both worked on
(hesitation) the President's…
campaign.

MATTHEW

Oh, right. The *President.*

PAUL

The President? So, you *do*
acknowledge that he won.
Hey, hey, hey! Progress.
Because the last time we
communicated there was a
bizarre stigmatization
process floating around.
(mournfully) And it's still out

there. Why, just the other
day, the President…

MATTHEW

The aforementioned *Il Duce-
bag*…

FAITH

Second warning! I'm gonna
get you to start singing
instead of bickering. Singing,
understand? No politics.
*(She heads back into the
kitchen trilling scales, and
the lights stay on in both
stage sections.)*

PAUL

She's worried that you're
going to explode.

MATTHEW

She's worried that *you're*
going to explode.

PAUL

Faith knows better. She
knows self-control comes
naturally to me. *(CANDY
pours him another glass of
wine and PAUL smiles.)*

MATTHEW

Seriously? Gee, Paul, I think we're going to have to cut you off from the *Amarone della Valpolicella – Classico*. Because, reviewing the greatest hits in your personal history of self-control, we'll have to include your kicking me out of your house on Christmas day because I questioned the efficacy of mixing Echinacea with vodka. Vodka! *(pours his own glass of wine)*

PAUL

(to CANDY) At the time, people were worried about mucus deposits spontaneously turning into the flu. So, people on the left started taking Echinacea straight up, which never worked, while conservatives took Echinacea with a chaser, which worked wonders. But Matty insisted

36

that Echinacea should never
be mixed with alcohol —
because that's what the CDC
said. Clowns.

MATTHEW

Refresh my memory: Your
medical degree is from what
school?

PAUL

A report in *The North
American Journal of
Enlightened Homeopathy*
proved that untreated
mucus deposits routinely
claimed twenty thousand
lives a year. Perhaps more.
(CANDY gasps)

FAITH

*(from the kitchen, where she
is chopping vegetables)* Are
we already on the
Echinacea? Congratulations,
boys: Seven minutes and
thirteen seconds before you
broke down and mentioned

those deadly mucus
deposits. A new personal
record. Now why don't you
turn those competitive
juices into something
positive, like finding some
sheet music?

(FAITH re-enters.)

CANDY

You two are wild! *(turning
to Faith)* Aren't they wild?

FAITH

(deadpan) Yes. Born to be
wild.

PAUL

(more agitated) Oh, you
should have seen him
standing up on the dining
room table at our parents'
house thirty years ago,
waving his library card and
lecturing us on the true
meaning of the word
"liberal" being connected to
the Latin "*liber*" for "book."
Which is wrong, by the way.

MATTHEW

I was joking.

PAUL

All in defense of... *(suddenly
clasps his chest and starts to
gasp)*

MATTHEW

It's okay to say *that* name,
although even I don't like
hearing it very much.
(actorly voice to CANDY)
Dukakis.

CANDY

Who was Dukaka?

MATTHEW

Famous Bay State tank
commander...

FAITH

*(While they converse, PAUL
appears to be having a heart
attack.)* Paul? Are you okay?

PAUL

Aargh!!!! Aargggh! *(He wobbles over to a
chair.)* This is what happens when...

MATTHEW

(They all react.) Christ. Are
you okay?

PAUL

Oh, Jesus...

CANDY

Paul, baby, breathe. Focus on your breath. *Pranayama.* Left nostril. Left nostril. *(CANDY tries to help him close one nostril, but he shakes himself away and rises from the chair, only to stagger to the kitchen door like Frankenstein's monster, where he supports himself against the doorframe, tenses his body, and then relaxes and turns back to them.)*

PAUL

Gas. *(waving his hand like a fan)* Acid reflux. My herbal supplement is supposed to handle it. Sorry. Happens without warning. And I always think it's a heart attack. One day it will be.

MATTHEW

Maybe gas *and* a heart attack? Get your money's worth, bro. I'd buy a ticket to see you go up in flames.

Like Brunhilde in
Gotterdammerung.

PAUL

Hopefully, you'll be right
there at my side, locked in
one final fraternal embrace.
Excuse me, the bathroom is
where...? *(PAUL exits
through the bathroom door
stage right.)*

CANDY

Oh, *mi corazon! (pats her
chest and sits)* So you teach
college?

MATTHEW

Part-time. Mostly, I write.
We run a small publishing
house.

FAITH

Very *small.* You can barely
see it.

CANDY

(to FAITH) And you do...?

MATTHEW

Faith manages the
publishing operations.

FAITH

I manage like it's going out
of style.

MATTHEW

We're a team.

FAITH

Go, team!

CANDY

That must be great. To be a
team. But how does that
work on a day-to-day basis?

FAITH

He pitches, and I catch.

*(A loud flush is heard, and
then PAUL emerges from the
powder room. He closes the
door with great ceremony.)*

PAUL

That was fantastic. The best.
Ohhhh. *(singing)* I feel good.
(continues to moan happily) I
knew that I would.

MATTHEW

Please accept our
congratulations, but could

we skip the proctology
report?

PAUL

(taking a seat) Why? If we
feel good, what's wrong with
spreading the news?

MATTHEW

Spreading the news about
your latest bowel
movement? *(CANDY pats
PAUL'S back.)*

PAUL

Why not? No need to stick to
the uptight liberal narrative.
We're in a new age now,
where you can talk about
anything, Matty. Well,
maybe not here in the
politically correct
demilitarized zone.

FAITH

Watch it!

PAUL

Harmless joshing.

FAITH

I better check on the food.
(to PAUL) We're having your

favorite dishes. Farro salad
with fried cauliflower and
prosciutto. *(As PAUL
applauds, FAITH turns to
CANDY.)* Okay with you?

CANDY

I eat everything. None of
that vegetarian, low-fat,
gluten-free crap for me.

PAUL

She's omnivorous.
Insatiable.

*(Seeing that
MATTHEW is
about to
challenge
CANDY, FAITH
grabs his arm.)*

FAITH

There is something I need
you to do.

PAUL

I can help.

FAITH & MATTHEW

No! *(They laugh.)*

FAITH

You're the guest. Relax.

(FAITH and MATTHEW enter the kitchen, where the lights come up dimly. MATTHEW mimes his distress and frustration, as FAITH seeks to calm him. Meanwhile, CANDY and PAUL stay in the living room.)

CANDY

Why didn't you tell them I was coming?

PAUL

I thought I did. *(She pours and hands him another glass of wine.)* Maybe not. An innocent mistake.

CANDY

I don't think so. *(grabs his shirt)* I think you wanted to fuck with their minds.

PAUL

(shaking his head and laughing) Not everyone is as diabolical as you, *mi alma.*

CANDY

But you are. You're always
fucking with people's minds.
Fucking and fucking and
fucking some more. *No es
verdad?*

PAUL

Stop it! I'd never do that. Not
with my family. We just like
to mix it up a bit.

CANDY

Triggering liberals. Fucking
with them. Fucking and re-
fucking. That's what you do.
You are a mind-fucker. A
total fucking mind-fucker.

PAUL

No, I'm not. At least not here.
Matty and Faith are family.
(She laughs.) Seriously. My
purpose is to persuade, not
degrade. *(She shakes her
head.)* I love my brother.
*(They kiss and a beat later,
as the light goes down in the
kitchen, MATTHEW enters
with more hors d'oeuvres.)*

CANDY

I'm going to get a refill.
That's very good bourbon.
(She exits to the kitchen.)

PAUL

*(PAUL takes some food and
motions for MATTHEW to sit
next to him, but MATTHEW
remains standing.)* How's
that small but well-
respected publishing house
of yours?

MATTHEW

Great. Fabulous. A few new
books coming out.
Promising titles. How about
you?

PAUL

Fantastic. Best year ever.
Almost done with my new
book delineating a foolproof
investment strategy in an
economy where things just
keep getting better and
better.

MATTHEW

Better and better than what?

PAUL

Than before. *(He stands.)*

MATTHEW

Paul, the economy's been booming for years.

PAUL

Define "booming." *(They are nose to nose.)*

FAITH

(from kitchen) What's going on in there?

MATTHEW

Paul is teaching me the principles of behavioral finance.

FAITH

(leading CANDY, who is holding her refilled glass of bourbon) We should sing. Before we eat. *(singing in a joking way)* Do-re-mi-fa-so-la-ti-do.

PAUL

And if we can't tell the truth
about the economy, I think
we'll also be singing after we
eat.

MATTHEW

But not *while* we eat, please.
(to CANDY) Does he still
keep running his mouth,
with the food spilling out all
over the place? Like Jabba
the Hut at Bob's Big Boy?

CANDY

You two are really alike.
You're so wild. Aren't they...
wild?

FAITH

Ask me again after you've
spent an evening with them.
Or, in my case, a half-
century.

PAUL

But if I might finish my
thought on the economy –
because the one
indisputable fact in all this is
that (pauses) *somebody* I

know is getting the job
done...

MATTHEW

And what exactly is *the job*?

PAUL

Managing the economy. Job
Number One.

MATTHEW

Please. President -- the last
guy -- deserves all the credit
for that. He saved us from a
second Great Depression. He
did. The only job your guy
ever managed was a hand
job. And he had to pay for
that.

FAITH

Stop it, Matthew! *(She
pushes him, then goes to the
drawer to fetch some sheet
music.)*

MATTHEW

(feigning innocence) But
Faith, don't you remember?
We're living in a brave new
world! A world where we
can talk about anything.

Literally anything. Bowel
movements. Hand jobs. Gas.
That's what Paul says.

FAITH

Just drop it, Matthew. You
too, Paul. Let's sing. *(FAITH
gives the brothers a few
pieces of sheet music.)*

MATTHEW

He started it.

PAUL

Did not.

FAITH

Oh, boy...

PAUL

I simply asked how your
boutique publishing house
was getting along. And
then...

FAITH

You know something? I quit
proctoring homeroom years
ago, boys. *(smacks them
both with the sheet music)*

CANDY

I couldn't teach children. No
way. Can't even be in the
same room with them for
more than five minutes.
Their needs are
inexhaustible.

MATTHEW

And yet you're with Paul?

FAITH

Are you two going to pick
fights with each other all
evening? C'mon, what's a
good harmony we all
remember?

CANDY

(ignoring her) Human beings
are hard-wired to fight, to
compete. Scientifically, it's in
our nature, and we shouldn't
deny our nature. Our
ancestors understood. They
were *hyper*-aware of
potential dangers lurking
out there.

MATTHEW

Like having their long-lost
brothers unexpectedly drop
by?

FAITH

(ignoring him) But the
human race has evolved.

CANDY

Isn't that just another
"progressive" myth? The
reality is, exactly like our
ancestors, we see threats
everywhere; *Es la realidad.*
We smell them; we taste
them. And when that
happens, our lizard brain
wants to rear up and strike.
(mimes striking)

FAITH

Our lizard brain?

CANDY

Biology rules. *Es la realidad.*

MATTHEW

Biology? Faith taught that
once upon a time. You two
could discuss — oh, I don't
know — whether dinosaurs
are more than six thousand
years old. Or climate change.

FAITH

No. Climate change is off the
table tonight. So is Medicare.
And taxes.

MATTHEW

What do you do, Candy?
Besides making sure Paul
takes his serotonin. *(FAITH
swats him with the sheet
music.)*

CANDY

(to FAITH) I like the way you
handle him. *(She pats PAUL
on the arm.)* I could learn a
few things. *(to MATTHEW)*
I'm a social media
consultant.

PAUL

Hey, hey, hey! Too modest.
University of Miami
Doctorate. International
Relations. And now she is a
platinum-level dissent
exterminator.

CANDY

Oooh, that sounds positively
evil. *(pause)* I like it.
(laughs) I'm going to add
that to my LinkedIn profile.

FAITH

Dissent exterminator?
Meaning...

PAUL

Meaning that if someone is
concerned about what
people are saying about
them online, or if they are
spreading quote, unquote
"fake news," she steps in and
obliterates them.

FAITH

How does she... *(to CANDY)*
you... do that?

CANDY

Trade secret. *(laughs)* No,
it's simple. And I don't need
any of those mysterious bots
you're always hearing about.
I work the trends and the
threads. Influence the
influencers. I merely supply
words as ammunition and
then watch the troops mow
down the enemy.

MATTHEW

Do you work for both sides?

CANDY

I work for the side that pays
the most for punishing the
treasonous. (*MATTHEW
starts to respond, but FAITH
jumps in.*)

FAITH

We should sing. Do you sing,
Candy?

CANDY

No, but I'm a terrific listener.
So, I'll just sit back and be
the impartial judge.

PAUL

(laughing and hugging her)
Hey, hey. It's not a
competition, babe. That's
not how music works. We
sing harmony. *Armonia*!

CANDY

Por supuesto. But really
everything is a competition,
even when you pretend that
it's not. That's basic biology.
Es la realidad.

MATTHEW

Fine. So, let's get right into it
with "All You Need Is Love."

CANDY

I adore that song. Katy
Perry, right?

FAITH

No, let's start with one of the
old Irish favorites your
mother loved. *(singing)* "I've
been a wild rover for many a
year..."

PAUL

(taking up his line) "And I
spent all my money on
whiskey and beer."

MATTHEW

"But now I'm returning with
gold in great store, and I
never will play the wild
rover no more."

FAITH, PAUL, MATTHEW

"And it's no, nay, never,
No, nay never no more;
Will I play the wild rover,
No never no more."

MATTHEW

No, no, no, no, no, wait a
minute! *(waving his hands to
stop them)* What part were
you singing, Paul?

PAUL

Wasn't I supposed to handle
the melody?

CANDY

You actually used to sing
songs like that? In public?
Madre de Dios. Why?

FAITH

We were folksingers. It's a
very famous folk song.

CANDY

Famous where?

PAUL

I've got an idea: Let's do
something *quintessentially*
American. *(blows on
pitchpipe and then sings)* "I
looked over Jordan and
what did I see, coming for to
carry me home?" *(The
others hesitate.)*

CANDY

A Negro spiritual! Yes! *(She hesitates.)* Perdonme. I did not mean to say "Negro."

FAITH

(FAITH picks it up.) "A band of angels coming after me, coming for to carry me home."

MATTHEW

Swing low, sweet chariot, coming for to carry me home." *(They look at each other and nod, the signal to start harmonizing.)*

FAITH, PAUL, MATTHEW.

"Swing low, sweet chariot, coming for to carry me home."

PAUL

Are we flat?

FAITH

Not to my ears.

CANDY

Ask about mine.

MATTHEW

Maybe we should warm up a
bit more. *(chugs a glass of
wine)*

FAITH

Oh, gosh, I've got to check on
the food. *(She runs out into
the kitchen.)*

CANDY

I'm going to go and pretend
to help. *(She kisses PAUL
lingeringly and leaves.)*

PAUL

Isn't she great? *No es la
verdad*? Having a girlfriend
like her makes me want to
live forever.

MATTHEW

Girlfriend? What, are you
still in high school??

PAUL

Okay, lady friend. Significant
other. No, I got it: *Mi cielito*.

MATTHEW

One to a customer, pal.
Which is it?

PAUL

Inamorata. (beat) And get this: We're moving in together.

MATTHEW

Ah, the classic Methuselah Finesse! Well, good luck with that, old timer! Especially with that bum ticker of yours.

(Lights switch to kitchen, where FAITH maneuvers ingredients in and out of the saucepan. CANDY leans in to watch.)

FAITH

I have to find the other saucepan, the big one. And the oil. Which has to get up to three-hundred-and-fifty degrees. And then I come in here every five minutes and switch out the batches.

CANDY

Do you miss your career — teaching?

FAITH

High school biology? That
wasn't a career. And being a
mother wasn't really a
career either. More like a
sentence: Hard labor with
no chance of parole. But I do
love my kids!

CANDY

So, you were a stay-at-home
mom?

FAITH

Back then, we just called it
"mom."

CANDY

That must've been so nice.
Traditional. Like on *Mad
Men*. Did your progressive
friends make you feel guilty
about that?

FAITH

Progressive friends? What
does that…//

CANDY

*(CANDY barrels straight
ahead.)* I read this study that
said that stay-at-home
moms are much more likely

to experience sadness or
anger or listlessness or
suicidal impulses during the
day than moms who work
outside the home making
lots of money and building
important careers. Was that
true for you?

FAITH

Depended upon the day. But
I'm generally a happy
person.

CANDY

What would get you angry?
Or make you feel intensely
suicidal?

FAITH

(moving some ingredients)
Excuse me, I have to slice
the *prosciutto. (She flashes a
very deliberate smile.)*

(The lights shift, and we see that Paul and Matthew, both seated, are drinking wine.)

PAUL

The new book is going to be big. Everyone needs a more sophisticated investment approach now that the new tax cut turned out to be so good.

MATTHEW

Good in what sense?

PAUL

In dollars and cents.

MATTHEW

I think there are times when paying taxes is the proper thing to do.

PAUL

Why? So, some fat, lazy bureaucrat can piss away your hard-earned money?

MATTHEW

Paul. Remember the rules of
engagement Faith set down?

PAUL

Faith isn't here. And this
isn't politics. It's...//

FAITH

(from the other room) I *can*
hear you. Start warming up.
Let me hear some lip trills
and flutters. *(She does some
trills, which elicits laughter
from them.)*

MATTHEW

I know a song that's perfect
for tonight. *(starts singing)*
"Once I built a railroad, I
made it run, made it race
against time. Once I built a
railroad, now it's done.
Brother, can you spare a
dime?"

PAUL

Oh, and *that's* keeping
politics out of the
conversation? Why not just

go ahead and sing the
Internationale?

CANDY

(*re-entering*) Oh, I know
that song. *(in a sing-song
fashion)* "Stand up, all
victims of oppression / For
the tyrants fear your
might! / Don't cling so hard
to your possessions. For you
have nothing if you have no
rights!" *(She cracks up
laughing.)*

MATTHEW

How do *you* know the words
to *the* socialist anthem?

CANDY

I learned it doing
undercover work in college.

PAUL

Isn't she amazing? She
infiltrated these leftist
groups filled with all of
these googly-eyed,
privileged trust-fund kids.

You know? Like the ones you lecture.

MATTHEW

Privileged? You mean like white privilege? Wouldn't that term also describe the avaricious swine who turn up at your personal-finance seminars? *(FAITH reenters.)* Another thing: Nobody uses expressions like "googly-eyed" anymore. You sound like Spiro Agnew.

FAITH

What are you talking about now?

PAUL

Cognitive therapy.

MATTHEW

Animal husbandry. *(They both laugh.)*

PAUL

Let's talk about your wonderful kids. How are they doing?

FAITH

Well, Beth is in her third
year of teaching.

CANDY

Smart girl! Retire at forty
and live off the rest of us for
the next fifty years.

PAUL

That said, a noble
profession.

FAITH

And Liz finished nursing
school in May.

PAUL

Healthcare isn't going to go
away even if... *(stops
himself)* Same boyfriend?

FAITH

Yes, and still *just* a
boyfriend.

PAUL

This generation is slower to
commit.

FAITH

Sad but true. And Edward?

PAUL

Hey, hey, hey. Good news
there. He just joined the
think tank that picked the
last three Supreme Court
justices, and now...//

MATTHEW

(changing the subject) Guys,
we're being rude. Talking
about family like this.
Leaving our guest on the
sidelines.

CANDY

It's fine. Families fascinate
me. *La familia es muy
importante. Muy.*

FAITH

Tell us about yours.

CANDY

I come from a strong Latino
family; lots of *familismo*. A
little too much right now. So,
we're taking some time off
from each other, to learn to
have more respect for each
other's life choices.

FAITH

I'm sorry to hear that.

CANDY

No, it's all good. *Familismo* is too intense. You're not allowed to have your own beliefs. But I love the *idea* of families. Especially other people's families. *(FAITH nods, noncommittally.)*

PAUL

I always thought of our friends as our extended family. They certainly showed up for Sunday dinner often enough. *(to MATTHEW)* Don't you miss that?

MATTHEW

Sunday dinner? Jesus, Paul, Mom died eighteen years ago. That's about a thousand Sundays. Sure, I still miss *her*, but her cooking? Are you nuts?

PAUL

What I meant was don't you miss those feelings of connection to our people?

MATTHEW

I'm still connected.

PAUL

Kind of the odd man out
now when it comes to the
people we grew up with.

MATTHEW

The *odd* man out?

PAUL

I'm just saying that within
our constellation of friends,
you're now an outlier
because of your views about
(pause) our current
President.

MATTHEW

What friends are you talking
about? *Your* friends? *Your*
friends? That would be the
first five people you meet in
hell. And the next five, too.

PAUL

At least I still have five
friends.

FAITH

(taking a drink) Let's try
another song.
"Shenandoah?" Your big
number, Paul.

CANDY

(pointing to watch) It's five
minutes.

FAITH

Oh, thank you.

CANDY

They say I'm a born
manager.

*(FAITH hustles to
kitchen, switches
the cauliflower
for the next
batch.)*

PAUL

Donnie Dryer was saying the
same thing last week...//

MATTHEW

Donnie was *your* friend. And
an enormous asshole.

CANDY

Wow! You really do speak
your mind. Not like some
progressives. *Bravo*!

PAUL

Donnie is my best friend,
Matthew.

MATTHEW

Goebbels was Hitler's best
friend. No, maybe it was
Goering. Hard to keep those
guys straight.

CANDY

I thought *I* was your best
friend.

PAUL

Of course, you are the best
of my best friends. *Lo mejor
de los mejores amigos.*

CANDY

Amigas. Feminine.

PAUL

*(singing) Amigas. Amiga.
Amante.* Whatever. *Que sera,
sera, non*?

FAITH

(returning) That's Italian,
Paul. But this conversation
is silly. We have no way of

knowing who our friends
voted for.

MATTHEW

Whom.

PAUL

I do. I make it my business
to find out where people
stand. And whether they've
changed. Ran into Pete
Schroeder down in Boca and
went right up and asked
him.

FAITH

And what did he say?

PAUL

He was for *him.* He was *all*
in.

MATTHEW

Pete? That's ridiculous.

PAUL

I only know what he told
me.

MATTHEW

What did he tell you? Let me
hear it. Verbatim.

PAUL

I'll try to be precise,
Professor. He said: "Paul,
when I got into that polling
booth, I just couldn't bring
myself to vote for *her*. Not in
good conscience."

MATTHEW

But he didn't actually say
that he voted for the Foul
Fiend, did he? Maybe he
penciled in Voldemort as a
write-in candidate. Or
maybe he was just humoring
you, the way he pretended
to enjoy Mom's Baked
Alaska. Which everybody
hated.

PAUL

Why would he humor me?

MATTHEW

Because he knows how bat-
shit you'd get if he dared to
disagree with you.

PAUL

Bat-shit? Hey, hey, hey!
Who's the one raising his
voice here? *(calming down)*
Seeing you so changed and
estranged from your own
people, it breaks my heart,
Matty. It really does.

MATTHEW

What heart? And who says
I'm estranged?

PAUL

Estranged from the people
we grew up with, people
who all understand what
needs to happen to put our
country back on track.
Tommy Farrell. Billy Snyder.
Mike Malloy.

FAITH

Hang on! Didn't Billy Snyder
die from pancreatic cancer?
In excruciating pain? *Before*
the last election?

PAUL

(sheepishly) Did he? Sorry to
hear that. But if he was still
alive, knowing Billy, you
know he'd vote for...

MATTHEW

(fake shock) You are
shameless. (to CANDY in a
spooky voice)
Gerrymandering the dead.

FAITH

What about Ed Mulligan? He
was one of your closest
friends. Mulligan voted for....

PAUL

Sad but true. I've had to put
that friendship on hold.

FAITH

You're not friends with Ed
anymore?

PAUL

No. We're through.

FAITH

Mikey McAuliffe?

PAUL

On hold. But there I still
have hopes.

CANDY

*Mientras haya vida, existe la
esperanza. (Hearing this, all*

three turn to face her.)
Where there is life, there is
hope.

FAITH

What about your old
girlfriend, that Polish girl?
What was her name?
Monica?

MATTHEW

Monica Petrowski.

CANDY

You had a girlfriend named
Monica Petrowski? Wild!
Sexy blonde?

PAUL

(shaking his head) Monica is
beyond being on hold.

CANDY

What I love about Paul is
that he sticks to his
principles.

MATTHEW

So did Jack the Ripper.

FAITH

(cuffs MATTHEW on the shoulder) But seriously, Paul: Ed and Monica? Those are dear old friends.

PAUL

Faith, how can I have a real conversation with them today? There's just too much hate. And not just for *(pause)* our President, but for everyone who supported him, all those good, hard-working Americans supporting The Fifth American Revolution. The title of my last book, by the way.

MATTHEW

Second choice, though. *Mein Kampf* was already taken.

PAUL

Oh, right, the classic, knee-jerk, holier-than-thou, East Coast liberal go-to move: Everyone who disagrees with you is a Nazi.

FAITH

Paul! He's joking. Don't
make it sound like we're
fighting the Civil War all
over again.

CANDY

In a way, we are. Except that
this time we're not fighting
about states' rights.

MATTHEW

We weren't fighting about
states' rights last time. We
were fighting about slavery.
You can look it up.

CANDY

Matthew, *por favor*, that's
just one narrow-band
version of American history.
(FAITH pinches MATTHEW.)
People like us are fighting
for individual rights today.
Individual freedom.

PAUL

(singing) Freedom!
Freedom! (speaking) *El
precio de la libertad es la
eternal vigilanticia.*

CANDY

(*corrects his mistake, but sweetly*) *Vigilancia*. And it's *eternale*.

PAUL

Claro. We were all raised to be prepared to fight for freedom. But somehow we've forgotten what the word "freedom" means. Concord and Lexington. Bunker Hill. Molly Pitcher! Why, I remember your father, Faith...//

FAITH

So do I. Proceed with caution.

PAUL

(to CANDY) Vinny was one of those tough Italian guys from Arthur Avenue. A Marine. Fought on Guadalcanal. *And* Iwo Jima. (to Faith) You know he would have voted for our guy.

FAITH

(interrupting) No, I don't know that! And in any case,

they're *my* people, not yours. Leave the dead out of this. *(upset)* Paul, you're breaking your promise.

PAUL

(after a pause, singing with a smile) Sorry. Sorry. Sorry. So, so, so sorry. (FAITH smiles reluctantly.)

FAITH

I need to turn over the cauliflower.

PAUL

(singing, tap-dancing) Don't turn over the cauliflower, with anyone else but me...

CANDY

Only one minute late. No, two. But I'm sure it will be fine. *(FAITH, exiting, stares at CANDY.)*

PAUL

(to the others, in a stage whisper) But her father would have!

MATTHEW

Stop being such an...

CANDY

Asshole? He can't help
himself. *(She tousles his
hair.]* He's just a big boy out
to have some fun. But he's
harmless. And such a good
person. You know that.

PAUL

*Yo estoy un hombre
sincero...*

CANDY

*(laughing a little and
correcting him) Yo soy.* The
verb *"ser"* is used to describe
a personality trait. Not
"estar."

MATTHEW

So, Candy, Paul now has his
own personal Spanish tutor
in you? *Caramba.*

PAUL

Actually, I keep up my
Spanish through my
business contacts: Latin-
American investors love a
little Spanglish. And now I
have a very good reason to
practice. By the way, how's
your French these days?

MATTHEW

(cartoonish accent) Me no
know; ask Pepe.

CANDY

(recoiling) That's quite the
racist stereotype, Matthew.
You surprise me.

MATTHEW

(flustered) I'm sorry. It's a
joke thing we used to say to
each other as kids.

CANDY

Is that supposed to make it
less offensive to Latinos?

MATTHEW

No. I meant that ... I
apologize...//

CANDY

(laughing) I'm playing you. I
don't care. It *is* funny. Trust
me, I'm not a PC girl.

PAUL

Candy, stop triggering my
helpless, hapless liberal
sibling. It's like teasing the
animals at the zoo.

CANDY

Yes. Particularly, the okapis.
So soft. So sensitive.

MATTHEW

I should go help Faith.

*(He exits to
kitchen; PAUL
follows him.
Lights come up.)*

PAUL

Actually, at some point I
wanted to get a couple
minutes alone with you to
discuss something personal,
Matty.

MATTHEW

Your funeral arrangements?
Mahogany or burnished
marble?

PAUL

(exasperated) Matty! There's
something I need to discuss
with you here...

MATTHEW

Okay, but let's wait until
after dessert. I think it's
Baked Alaska. (*silence, as*

FAITH keeps working on the food)

PAUL

What's wrong? You seem so uptight.

MATTHEW

This *(gestures around the room)* whole thing makes me uncomfortable.

PAUL

Well, it doesn't make me uncomfortable. Not at all.

MATTHEW

That's why it *does* make me uncomfortable. Because it *should* make you uncomfortable.

FAITH

Matthew. Not now. Not in the kitchen. Too many sharp objects.

PAUL

We're just having a conversation. Like we used to talk late at night as kids. You remember those nocturnal *tête-à-têtes*.

MATTHEW

Paul, we haven't had a
conversation in years. We go
directly from third-degree
interrogation to insults to
brainwashing.

PAUL

Because I support our
President? Hey, hey, hey! I
didn't stop talking to you
when *your* guy was in the
White House.

MATTHEW

You *didn't* talk *to* me; you
talked *at* me — endlessly
and apoplectically. And I
wasn't part of a hate-filled
movement led by *(pause)*
your... *your...//*

FAITH

Cut it out, both of you.

PAUL

Hate? My side is filled with
hate? I'm the hater? Hey,
hey, hey, I think we need a
little fact-check here.

*(PAUL rushes
first to the living
room, and then
exits the house
completely.)*

FAITH

He was just trying to talk,
Matthew! You don't have
one ounce of self-control...//

MATTHEW

He started it.

FAITH

Mary, Mother of God! What
are you, eight? *(She goes
into the other room where
CANDY sits by herself.)*
Where did he go?

CANDY

Outside. Not being able to
express himself is very
difficult for my Pablito
Bonito.

FAITH

A McCarthy brother not
being able to express
himself? *Madonn'*! These
two lollapaloozas do nothing
but express themselves. And
your personal lollapalooza
promised not to talk about
politics, period. He
promised.

CANDY

That was a ridiculous
promise. No one could
expect him to honor that.

FAITH

If he knew he couldn't honor
it, then it wasn't a promise.

CANDY

Aren't promises made to be
broken?

(FAITH stares at her. MATTHEW enters from the kitchen. PAUL storms through the front door, waving a lawn sign.)

PAUL

Hey, hey, hey! What have we here? *(He adopts an actorly voice, positioning sign in front of him.)* "Hate has no home here." *"El odio no tiene hogar aquí."* *(Looks to CANDY for pronunciation approval and points to the characters on the sign, written in Arabic, Hebrew, and Korean.)* Blah, blah, blah: Hate has no home here. *(holds sign closer)* What? No Yoruba? No Swahili? How will the Senegalese know that this is a safe house? Not to mention the Namibians. As usual, the poor Namibians get left out

in the cold. And that's just
not fair.

CANDY

Such bullshit. Where is this
so-called racism and
oppression you complain
about? Fake problems.
Manufactured.

PAUL

Hate has no home here? You
and your socialist comrades
hate our current president,
hate our vice president, *hate*
the Senate Majority
Leader...//

MATTHEW

You left out the Secretary of
Commerce. And the House
whip.

PAUL

We know you despise half
the country.

MATTHEW

(speaking over PAUL)
Technically, it's more like

forty-two-point-four percent. And no, we are not haters. We just don't like you.

PAUL

(roaring back and waving the sign) Cut the crap. Hate doesn't just have a home here, little brother. It's the state religion of your precious little People's Republic of Montclair.

FAITH

Paul, that's our neighbor's lawn sign. Put it back.

PAUL

Hold on a sec; why don't *you* have one, Matty? Are you tacitly admitting that hate *does* have a home here? That *el odio* does *tiene* un *hogar alli*?

CANDY

(correcting him) Aqui, Paul. Not *alli*. It's true, though. You must be the only ones in the neighborhood without a sign.

MATTHEW

(sheepishly) The supplier ran out; it's on back-order.

PAUL

What the signs are really saying is: *I'm* not welcome here. And *Candy's* not welcome here. *(shaking the sign some more)* Between the lines, the message is that anyone who disagrees with you elitist, leftist, gender-fluid, LGBTQ, emotionally fragile love-bunnies is a subhuman criminal.

MATTHEW

We're fragile? *We're* fragile? How emotionally "fragile" is someone if a flimsy piece of cardboard delivers a death blow to his ego? Someone puts up a sign in a couple of mildly exotic foreign languages and all of a sudden the alt-right is alt-wronged?

PAUL

(moving forward, still carrying the sign waist-high) Alt-right? You're calling me...

FAITH

(at a high volume, singing)
"There is a house in New
Orleans..." *(motioning to
them to pick up the tune, but
they do not join in)* "...they
call the Rising Sun." *(gives
up)* Oh, come on. I'm going
to make you shut up and
sing or I'm going to die
trying. And speaking of
dying, Paul, if you don't put
that sign back, the guy next
door is going to murder us.
You're twisting it and
smearing it and our
neighbor is going to be very
upset if that sign is
damaged. Whether you like
it or not, it's his property.

CANDY

(taking the sign) Let me have
it, *mi amor*. I'll take care of it.
(She exits.)

FAITH

Paul, what did we talk about
on the phone?

PAUL

You mean the... *(gestures at
MATTHEW)*

FAITH

No. That too, but I mean
your promise that this
would be an evening of
singing and eating and
drinking and then more
singing. Fat chance! Now, I
feel trapped, like a
passenger in a car with two
drunk drivers.

PAUL

It doesn't feel good for me
either, Faith.

MATTHEW

Finally, common ground: We
all feel like shit. Well, *(holds
out his hand)* thanks for
stopping by, Paul.

FAITH

No. There's something else.
(beat) Paul, tell him how you
were going to offer one of
your investment books to
our publishing house, and
let us have a best-seller for a
change.

MATTHEW

What? *His* book published
by *us*?

PAUL

Yes, *The Paul McCarthy Boot Camp: Thirty Days to a Richer, Richer, Richer, Richer You.* I'm literally gifting you a bestseller, Matty.

FAITH

The food! *(She rushes to the kitchen.)*

MATTHEW

Gifting? Faith, what did you two...? *(PAUL'S phone erupts with a jubilant salsa ring.)*

PAUL

That's Candy. *(into phone)* Que pasa, querida? *(His face contorts.)* Hey, hey, hey! Calm down. Where are you? Candy? Candy? *(PAUL rushes to the door.)*

MATTHEW

(grabbing him) What happened?

PAUL

What kind of a neighborhood is this? She's being arrested. *(FAITH enters from the kitchen,*

*holding a pan. First PAUL
and then MATTHEW head
out the door.)*

FAITH

Arrested? *(deciding which
way to go, looks up to
heaven, arms outstretched)*
Madonn'! A little help,
please? *(She heads out the
door, still clutching the
frying pan.)*

(END OF ACT I)

ACT II

*(PAUL and MATTHEW sit in
chairs. They are somber.
Faith comes through the
outside door and closes it
with a slam.)*

FAITH

Jesus, Mary and Joseph. *(shakes her
head at them)* Okay, it's all sorted out.
The cops are explaining it to the
neighbors. *(She looks around.)* Candy's
in the powder room?

PAUL

Putting Neosporin on the
handcuff bruises.

MATTHEW

Makes sense. She *is* a neo-
conservative. *(PAUL glares.)*

FAITH

If you two start arguing
about politics again, I'll
break that goddamn *White
Album* over both of your
thick heads. Talk business.
*(FAITH goes into the kitchen.
MATTHEW nods and then*

stares at PAUL for a second before following Faith determinedly. The lights come up there and dim in the living room. While FAITH slices prosciutto, MATTHEW hovers. She speaks first.) Did you want to say something?

MATTHEW

(loud whisper) Do I want to say something? Yes, I want to say a lot of things, but for now one word will suffice: humiliating!

FAITH

Humiliating?

MATTHEW

Yes, humiliating. Degrading. Debasing. Embarrassing. Infuriating.

FAITH

With you, that one-word limit never lasts very long.

MATTHEW

You want one word? Okay, here it is: Humiliating. Or did I already say that?

FAITH

I find that word quite useful,
too. Humiliating. As in, it's
"humiliating" that my
husband is happy to
describe our company as a
small publishing house. Hi,
I'm Matt. This is Faith. And
we run a *small* publishing
house. That's right, a *small*
publishing house. Just a wee
affair. In fact, to be
absolutely precise, we run a
tiny publishing house.
Microscopic. Unicellular.
America's most respected,
most admired, protozoan
publisher.

MATTHEW

Look, Faith...

FAITH

Why is *that* not humiliating?
Or maybe we could switch it
up once in a while. Like we
run "a one-step-ahead-of-
the-electric-company-
shutting-off-the-power-

publishing house?" *Maison Sisyphus*.

MATTHEW

I know that you're frustrated…

FAITH

You do? Then why don't you *do* something about it? Because whenever *I* try to do something about it …//

MATTHEW

How would you like it if *I* went behind *your* back to negotiate a deal like this?

FAITH

I'd *love* it. *Love* it. Knock yourself out. *(offers him the long knife)* You know what, just go ahead and kill me, because I can't take this crap anymore. Here. Be my guest. *(He throws his hands up and she resumes slicing.)*

MATTHEW

That's unfair.

FAITH

Unfair? You know what's
unfair? I never get to
introduce us as having a
medium-size publishing
house! Or God forbid, a
large, successful,
enormously profitable
publishing house?

MATTHEW

I'm sorry. I understand how
you feel. But asking Paul...//

FAITH

He asked me. And I said yes.
Because for one fleeting
moment, this glorious vision
came to me of growing the
business just enough that
maybe, just maybe, you
could hire someone else to
do your scut work, and I
could go out and do
something I actually want to
do.

MATTHEW

What *do* you actually want
to do?

102

FAITH

(louder) Unclear. But not this. Maybe I'll give singing lessons, since today's choir practice is going so well. *(She slams down the plate.)* Oh, God! How many ways can you find of getting your own way, Matthew? All I'm asking is for you to just talk to him.

MATTHEW

So, even if it means getting down on my hands and knees and begging my insane, crypto-fascist brother for help, that's what you want me to do?

FAITH

Well, gee, now that you put it that way — yes! Go fix this mess you made.

MATTHEW

Mess I made? *You* invited him. When you bring the circus to town, don't act

surprised by all the elephant
shit.

*(MATTHEW exits
to the living
room. The lights
go with him.)*

MATTHEW

How are you doing?

PAUL

I'm disturbed, Matty.
Unbelievable. Overreach and
overreaction.

MATTHEW

You stole the sign, Paul.

PAUL

Candy didn't.

MATTHEW

Candy didn't. And yes, she
was handcuffed. And yes,
that's horrible. But what is
the cop supposed to think,
seeing her pounding the sign
into the ground? With her
boot. On the wrong
neighbor's lawn.

PAUL

Or, as you liberals might put it, she was guilty of being a brown-skinned woman in a lily-white, upper-middle class, *progressive* neighborhood. Where your neighbor's a racist asshole. How's that for irony?

MATTHEW

Here's the thing, Paul: *You* stole his fucking sign. *You* broke the law. And then you have the nerve to cry "victim." How's that for irony?

FAITH

(*from kitchen*) How you doing in there, Matthew?

MATTHEW

Just educating my big brother.

PAUL

Yeah, he's delivering his freshman lecture on irony, Faith.

(CANDY returns.)

CANDY

When did everybody start
talking about irony all the
time? I know it was before I
was born. What *is* this
irony?

MATTHEW

Hmm, where to start? I
guess with the Greeks: *eírōn,*
actually a kind of character
in Greek comedy...//

CANDY

Is it "ironic" *(air quotation
marks)* that a Latina who is
actually an honorary sheriff
in Dade County gets
harassed by two goober
cops in a sanctuary city?

PAUL

Sanctuary village.

CANDY

Is it ironic that bleeding
heart, lefty, sensitive, caring
intellectuals turn out to be
the most incredible
hypocrites ever? Because
while they're busy sobbing

into their low-fat, shade-grown *chai lattes* over the plight of the underprivileged, a real-life person of color is getting wrongfully arrested right next door.

PAUL

To me, it's a sign of just how polarized the left has made...//

CANDY

No, Pablo. Here it's okay, because I am a Republican.

MATTHEW

They didn't know that. Anyway, *they're* Republicans. The cops. I think *that* might actually be ironic.

CANDY

Why?

MATTHEW

They voted for *your* guy.

CANDY

You're actually claiming that *all* cops vote Republican?

MATTHEW

In this solar system, yes. Just
like all choreographers vote
Democratic.

FAITH

(from the kitchen) Can
someone in there please set
the table?

*(PAUL and MATTHEW
rise and approach the
foldout table, but each
of them is taking a
different approach to
opening it and there is a
whole rigmarole around
setting it up until
CANDY waves them
aside and flips open the
leaves of the table.)*

CANDY

I can set the table. Worked
as a waitress in high school.

MATTHEW

So, just like us, you come
from a working-class
background. *(dragging a
chair over to the table)* And
yet...

PAUL

What's that supposed to
mean?

MATTHEW

Nothing. I'm merely
noting....

CANDY

No, you're profiling! Being
Hispanic with a solid blue-
collar background, you're
wondering why I am not a
liberal. Because that's what
liberals, with their autopilot,
just-add-water opinions
always do. *Latina*. Working
class. College-educated.
Must be a Democrat. But —
que sorpresa! — I'm not.

PAUL

Oh, I love it. I just love it!
You've caught my brother in
a bias incident. Reckless
stereotyping. Federal
offense. Twenty-five to life!
*(dragging second chair to
the table)* Bailiff, please
escort the prisoner out of
the courtroom.

FAITH

(sticking her head in) Once
again, I hear politics. And
that is *prohibito.*

PAUL

This isn't politics, Faith. It's
sociology. No, psychology.

*(CANDY and PAUL
laugh heartily.
FAITH enters with
dishes and
silverware all in a
basket. CANDY sets
the table speedily
and then starts to
roll napkins
elaborately.)*

FAITH

In that case, I'm expanding
the ban: No sociology. No
psychology. No ologies,
period. Get it?

PAUL

Just want you to be happy,
Faith, darling.

FAITH

Good. We have a few
minutes; I had to redo the
batch that burned while I
was next door playing public
defender. We're lucky that
the cop's wife is in my
Pilates class. Now we sing.
Before we drink too much.

MATTHEW

(singing suddenly) "This land
is your land..." (PAUL makes
noises of protest.)

FAITH

We used to sing that one a
lot.

(PAUL shakes his
head.)

MATTHEW

(to PAUL) Okay, what do you
want to sing? the Russian
national anthem? (PAUL
shuffles through the pile of
sheet music that FAITH had
placed on the sideboard.)
Let's do your new boss
Putin's personal favorite.
(He sings dramatically.)
"Ochi chyornye, ochi

zhguchie, Ochi strastnye..."
(FAITH muffles him with
sheet music.)

PAUL

Hey, hey, hey! "This Land Is
Your Land" *is* a political
song, and you said no
politics.

MATTHEW

Political? Are you kidding
me?

CANDY

Wasn't he a *comunista*, the
guy who wrote that song?
Some people say that he
meant it to be subversive.
(pause) It's what some
people say.

PAUL

He *was* a communist. It's a
fact. So was Pete Seeger. His
mother founded the
American Communist Party.

FAITH

Jesus, Paul, we must've sung
that song a thousand times...

PAUL

The mistakes of youth. Back then, I didn't realize that folk music was a linchpin in the great communist conspiracy. *(FAITH and MATTHEW suppress giggles.)* And the whole time we all joked about it, the damage to our great nation was being done — right before our ... ears.

CANDY

This is true. I read about it. In *National Review*. Maybe *The American Spectator.*

FAITH

Your day-care center subscribed to *National Review?* Wow.

CANDY

Paul has educated me. About the past. *(FAITH pinches MATTHEW before he speaks.)*

PAUL

That stuff got into the
movies, TV, even the
schools.

MATTHEW

And this was the Russians
who did all this? The same
Russians who helped
Illegally Blond win the
election?

PAUL

(interrupting) Communists.
Not Russians. Two different
things. Very different. And,
Matty, there was no
collusion!

FAITH

So, what can we sing*?*
(steadily, more forcefully)
Because I've got to get back
into the kitchen, so as far as
I'm concerned it can be
doleful Trans-Carpathian
folksongs. But we *will* sing.

*(A vigorous
knock shakes the
door. All stare as
MATTHEW opens
it. JERRY, tall,
gorgeous, forty-
something,
rushes in,
spreads his arms,
and kneels before
CANDY.)*

JERRY

I am beside myself. Words
fail me. *Siento lo que
ocurrido. Soy un montón ...
de duelo...*

CANDY

*(clutching her heart, quite
affected) No te preocupes, no
es nada.*

JERRY

*Dios mío, espero que no estés
herido de ninguna manera.
Me disculpo por...//*

PAUL

What's he saying? Candy?

MATTHEW

Yeah, *que pasa?*

CANDY

He wants to know if I was
hurt in any way. This man is
apologizing to me in the
most highly poetic fashion in
Spanish, the loving tongue.
*(to JERRY) Acepto tu
hermosa disculpa.*

FAITH

(to JERRY) What's up with
the Spanish, Jerry?

MATTHEW

(to PAUL) Offer one ESL
class and the next thing you
know the whole
neighborhood starts living
la vida loca.

CANDY

(To JERRY) Let's speak
English. For their sake.

MATTHEW

Somewhat awkward, but I'd
like to introduce our
neighbor Jerry to Candy and
my brother Paul.

116

(JERRY affects the air of a noble caballero approaching CANDY, taking her hand, and lightly, gallantly kissing it. He then rises from his knees and shakes hands with PAUL.)

FAITH

Where did you learn Spanish like that, Jerry? You are full of surprises.

JERRY

Peace Corps. (emphasizing his pronunciation) *Ni-ca-ra-gua.*

CANDY

Tu hablas español como un Madrileno.

JERRY

Tu español es como un poema!

PAUL

What did he say? I missed some of that.

CANDY

I told him that he speaks Spanish like a native. And he said to me *(gesturing to JERRY who smiles gallantly)* "My Spanish is like a poem." *(She swoons, perhaps a little too dramatically.)*

JERRY

Que linda! You remind me of a line from one of my favorite poems. *"Por contemplar tus ojos negros, ¿qué daría yo?*

CANDY

¡Auroras de carbunclos irisados abiertas frente a Dios!" (MATTHEW and FAITH swerve and look over at PAUL.)

MATTHEW

You can translate that, right, Paul? *Vamos, muchachos*!

PAUL

(annoyed, floundering)
"Looking at some black
eyes... iridescent
carbuncles... getting right in
God's face..." (CANDY and
JERRY laugh.)

CANDY

It's Lorca. I adore Lorca. (He
gestures to her eyes.) "My
dark eyes... dawns of
iridescent garnet." Eres muy
simpatico, Jerry. (to PAUL)
Don't you agree, Paul?

MATTHEW

Lorca? The Lorca who was
tortured and killed by the
fascists? And I mean really
tortured. That Lorca?

FAITH

No using the 'F' word today.

MATTHEW

I'm just saying, Lorca is on
our team. You guys don't get
Lorca. You can have Ezra
Pound.

JERRY

(recognizing PAUL) Paul?
Oh, my God! You are *that*
Paul McCarthy. *(to
MATTHEW)* You didn't tell
me you had a famous
brother! Of course, it all
makes sense now: You're
both in the world of
publishing!

FAITH

Sort of.

JERRY

(to PAUL) We watch your
show on FOX Business all
the time. In fact, it's the *only*
show we watch on Fox.
We've been following all of
your amazing investment
predictions ever since that
article about you came out
in the *Journal* last year.

MATTHEW

They must have laid off the
fact-checker that month.
(FAITH pinches him.)

CANDY

(chuffed that Jerry is praising her partner) Genio, verdad?

JERRY

Si, cierto! The man can certainly pick his stocks. And his women. *(CANDY fake-swoons again.)* But what brings you all together here today?

FAITH

Just a nice, quiet family meal and some lighthearted singing.

JERRY

You sing? *(to FAITH)* You never told me!

CANDY

They were in a group. They performed in those dark little coffee houses that you see in the movies. *(snaps her fingers like a beatnik)* Like real cool, daddy-o!

JERRY

Well, I'd love to stay for the concert *(sniffing)* and the food, and the charming company, but I just came over to apologize. So, I guess I'll say *"Adios. Es tan corto el amor y tan largo el olvido."*

CANDY

Neruda! "Love is so short and forgetting so long." Very beautiful — for a communist.

MATTHEW

Neruda is also on our team. He plays left. Stop poaching.

PAUL

I appreciate the apology, Jerry. Maybe next time, check things out a bit more thoroughly before you call the cops.

CANDY

And before I get arrested.

MATTHEW

Detained.

JERRY

I didn't call the cops.

PAUL

Well, then, who did?

JERRY

My husband Archer. Don't
get me started. *El puede ser
un dolor de huevos.*

CANDY

Huevos? Or *cojones*!

JERRY

(CANDY cracks up again.) A
pain in the ass. Pardon my
French.

*(FAITH ushers
him to the door.)*

FAITH

Well, all's well that ends
well. It's so nice that you
came over, Jerry.

JERRY

*(not picking up on the hint to
leave)* Archer can overreact
a little. *(to CANDY)* "*Una
reina del drama.
Verdamente.*"

CANDY

(cracking up) Oh, you are
just wild, Jerry. *(noticing
that the others are not
getting the joke)* He called
him a drama queen*! (to
JERRY)* How would your
husband feel about your
saying that?

JERRY

Oh, Archer doesn't speak
Spanish. *(FAITH still
ushering him to the door)*

PAUL

Does your husband just sit
by the window all day
keeping guard over your
sign?

JERRY

No. But he does keep an eye
out if he hears something.
We had some vandalism
issues in this neighborhood
last Halloween. Someone
urinated all over the signs.
Can you imagine?

PAUL

How sad for you! And for
Archer! *Lo siento. Lo siento
mucho.*

FAITH

But your sign is okay?

JERRY

Yes. I mean, it's just a sign.
Though it is an original from
the very first printing out in
Illinois, where that
precocious, albeit autistic,
kindergartner first came up
with the idea. Archer says
it's a collector's item, but I'm
like: "If it's such a precious
collectible, why are we
putting it out on the front
lawn?"

FAITH

Well, Jerry, the crisis has
passed. Now...

JERRY

(still not taking the hint) I
should've known that none
of you would ever
deliberately do anything bad
to our sign. It's just that we
freak out a little when we

125

see strangers in the neighborhood.

PAUL

It happens down by us, too. They come in, they walk around, they see what they like, and then they just take it.

JERRY

Who is "they?"

MATTHEW

I think it's "Who are they?" And I know *we* don't want to go there.

CANDY

The people who steal things. *Los ladrones.*

FAITH

Come on. I doubt that anyone could get past the guardhouse in your gated community anyway.

MATTHEW

Not to mention the nineteen-foot wall, topped by barbed wire and broken glass. With four machine-gun turrets.

JERRY

You live in a gated community?

MATTHEW

Not the kind you think. The gates are there to keep *him* in. *(makes the crazy sign)* I'm embarrassed to admit it, but Paul had to apply for a 48-hour pass before he could come visit us.

PAUL

Yes, the People's Undemocratic Republic of Montclair requires those of us from the real America to show our papers.

JERRY

I'm confused. *What* Republic?

CANDY

Son fieras, estos dos. *(to PAUL)* I told him you're wild.

FAITH

Brothers, Jerry. Irish guys.
From the Bronx. Teasing is a
sign of affection.

JERRY

I'm glad somebody can still
show some affection,
because mostly this country
is a mess. A hot mess. We
are *so* divided.

PAUL

And why do you think that
is, Jerry?

JERRY

Because no one can let go of
old grudges. *(to MATTHEW)*
It's just like that prayer
Matthew says at
Thanksgiving — except the
opposite. Everyone is like:
"Oh Lord, please *don't* take
this grudge from me, make it
bigger, make it 24/7, and
make it angry every waking
moment of the day and
twice as loud in my dreams."

PAUL

But no grudges for you, I
assume.

JERRY

I learned during a *challenging* adolescence to just offer them up and blow them away. Like our sign says: Hate has no home here.

PAUL

But what about honest disagreements? Do they have a home here? Just because you disagree with someone doesn't mean that you hate them.

FAITH

(She opens door.) We should eat.

CANDY

You just pity them. For they are sad.

PAUL

What those signs end up doing is labeling people like me as being hateful and ignorant...//

MATTHEW

Truth in advertising.

JERRY

I'm not labeling anybody.
The sign just says that it's a
safe place here.

CANDY

It comes across as virtue
signaling.

FAITH

Virtue signaling? What on
earth is that?

MATTHEW

It's like smoke signals, but
with much lower carbon
emissions.

PAUL

(ignoring him) It's people
showing off their virtue like
they show off their Priuses
and their fancy, oversized,
designer compost bins.
Showing how morally
superior you are so that the
other side — us — get the
message that we are the
scum of the earth, the
deplorables.

JERRY

Come on. All we did was put
up a nice sign.

PAUL

I mean, what's the median
house price in this town? A
million? A million-two? Who
exactly is unsafe here? I
didn't see any oppressed
people out on the street.

CANDY

Except for me. When they
cuffed me.

FAITH

Paul, we need to...//

JERRY

We're not saying that *we* are
the oppressed. We're saying
that we are fighting for *the*
oppressed.

PAUL

How exactly do you do that,
Jerry? An extra twenty in the
envelope at Christmas?
Leave out some leftovers
when the Frito Banditos
come over to clean?

CANDY

Banditas. Feminine.
Concentrate.

FAITH

Paul, that term is quite
offensive.

PAUL

So is the sign. To people like
me, *(to Jerry)* which I guess
is what you and/or your
husband intended.

MATTHEW

(to Faith) My, this is going
well.

PAUL

You know who is hated? The
people who you insist must
throw out their honored
traditions and stuff them
inside your color-coded
recycling bins. People like
us. *(He gestures to CANDY
and himself.)*

JERRY

Oh, my God: you're one of
them. You're on the dark
side. God, I can't believe that
we watch your show. And to

think: Archer bought *all*
your books!

MATTHEW

Which were *not* put out by a
small, well-thought-of
publishing house, by the
way.

CANDY

If people want to have their
signs, let them have their
stupid signs.

JERRY

(to PAUL) What sign would
you like? "You are now
entering Unpleasantville"?
"Welcome to Vigilante
Vistas?" I guess that would
please President...

FAITH

(FAITH quickly places her
hand over JERRY'S mouth
and caresses his back.) We
have agreed not to say that
name today.

PAUL

Exactly what can *we* say?
What kind of sign could *I* put
up that would convey that

same message 🕐 namely,
that I am *so* much better
than everybody else? (*PAUL
seizes the* White Album *and
pulls a pen from his pocket
and proceeds to create his
own sign in Spanish.*) *"Estoy
una persona mucho mejor
que tú. ¡De verdad!"* (*PAUL
hands the album to JERRY,
who gently takes the pen
from him and corrects the
wording*)

JERRY

Soy, not *estoy*. Common
mistake.

PAUL

I don't think so. "*Yo soy*"
means... (*CANDY shakes her
head and he shuts up.*)

JERRY

(*strained, to FAITH and
MATTHEW*) I came over
here to say I'm sorry, and I
should leave before I say
something else. "*Somos
buenos seres humanos. Eso
es suficiente.*" (*He kisses
CANDY'S hand and walks
out, studiously not slamming
the door. They all look over
to CANDY.*)

134

CANDY

"We are good human beings.
That's enough."

MATTHEW

*(He picks up the White
Album that JERRY had
slammed down and
addresses FAITH.)* Guess I
won't be getting two
thousand bucks for this on
eBay.

PAUL

By the way, *(patting his
chest)* in case anyone wants
to know how I'm doing, that
is, the guy who thought he
was having a heart attack an
hour ago, and who now had
the gay Caballero bursting
into the house, shamelessly
flirting with my *inamorata*
and...//

CANDY

Oh, *querida*! That's so nice.
But I think you mean
"*amada.*" Seriously, are you
okay? I mean with your
heart or your gas?

PAUL

I'm okay. I've gotten used to
feeling under attack.
(finishes the bottle of wine
by pouring what is left into
his glass)

MATTHEW

Under attack? You've been
on the offensive from the
moment you walked in the
door.

PAUL

Hey, hey, hey, hey...hey! For
eight long years we all had
to shut up and listen to your
"hopey changey" thing. Now
it's our turn. Payback's a
bitch, Matty.

MATTHEW

We shut you up? You ranted
so much about how you
hated the President, that is,
the ex-President, that is, the
person of color who was
formerly in the White
House...

PAUL

Bullshit. You people think
everything is a threat to
your safe space. You want to
turn the entire society into
the quiet car. Well, screw
that.

CANDY

The lizard brain again. On
steroids.

FAITH

Basta! Madonn'! What will it
take to get you guys to stop?
I'm not eating dinner while
all this settling of scores is
going on.

PAUL

I understand. Believe me, I
know what it's like to try
eating your dinner while
you're getting screamed at
in restaurants just because
of the hat you're wearing.

CANDY

And sometimes spit on. With
great vehemence.

137

MATTHEW

I love the idea of you as a
victim. Maybe you should
sue for reparations. You
could use the money to buy
a classier hat.

CANDY

Wait a minute. *(holds out
wrists)* Have you forgotten I
was a victim out there, just
doing the right thing?

FAITH

Oh, honey, don't you think
there's a difference between
someone making a mistake
and someone making you a
victim?

*(JERRY bursts in
again, rushing
straight over to
PAUL MATTHEW
and FAITH edge
closer to
intervene.)*

JERRY

There's just one thing I need
to know from *you*, Mister
Paul McCarthy. Was the
insulting behavior you just
threw my way triggered by

138

your political beliefs? Or
was it flat-out homophobia?
Or was it rage at my being
black? Or was it because I'm
Jewish? Politics, I can accept.
All my mother's people
voted for...// (*Faith covers
his mouth again and hugs
him.*)

MATTHEW

A corrupt, depraved, serial
sex offender and
pathological liar. With
thoroughly implausible hair.
(to FAITH) No names.

FAITH

Jerry, why did you come
back? I'm only here because
I live here.

JERRY

Faith, darling, I have learned
to *never* let anti-Semitism
and homophobia and
cultural profiling go
unanswered. Never. And I'll
tell you why. Because *un
pueblo unido jamas sera
vencido.*

CANDY

(*PAUL looks to her for
translation.*) No. I don't
translate Che.

MATTHEW

That was Allende. But it's
still time to get the women
and children off the playing
field. *(Again, he tries to
usher JERRY out of the
house.)*

PAUL

Point of order, *camarada*.
How would I even know that
you're Jewish?

JERRY

Please! The two of you are
from New York City. You
instinctively know who's
Jewish — even if it's a
convert like me.

CANDY

Isn't that some kind of
reverse bigotry, *primo*?

JERRY

No, it's called common
knowledge, *princesa*.

PAUL

Well, *I* didn't know. I *did*
know you were…
(*struggling*) gay. But I didn't
need to be from New York to
pick up on that.

JERRY

How very perceptive of you.

PAUL

But that doesn't matter to
me. I love gays. In fact, in my
line of work I much prefer
them to straight old guys.
Smarter. Funnier. Less
bullshit.

MATTHEW

Yeah, sure, Paul the
Smashing Pumpkin
Republican. Progressive to
the core.

CANDY

But he *does* love gay people.
When I first met *mi Pablito*, I
thought he might be gay
because he hung out with so
many flaming old queens.
And he took me to see Cher.
Twice.

PAUL

(to CANDY) I thought you liked Cher. *(to JERRY)* I swear that there is nothing personal in what I said to you. It's purely political.

JERRY

(After a long pause, during which he looks PAUL up and down) Was that an apology? Okay, I accept it, I think. But I could never forgive someone for being the very quintessence of evil.

FAITH

That's a very sensible attitude, Jerry. *(trying to usher him out)*

CANDY

I love the word "quintessence." This concept does not exist in Spanish. Not that I know of.

JERRY

So, Paul, we agree to disagree. *(He extends hand, but Paul spreads his hands.)*

PAUL

No, we *don't* agree to
disagree. If we agree to
disagree, what was the point
of disagreeing in the first
place?

CANDY

Paul, in this climate, I think...

MATTHEW

Ah, climate. Deft change of
subject.

PAUL

Rather than agreeing to
disagree, I think that we
should continue to disagree
until such time that you
finally realize — as I'm sure
you will — that...

JERRY

That you are an
unbelievable asshole? I'm
there, *camarada*. I am *so*
there. *(They are poised to
fight.)*

CANDY

Paul!

FAITH

Jerry! *(MATTHEW steps between them.)*

MATTHEW

Okay, block party is over.

FAITH

(visibly upset) Please. This is my house. Paul, what were you thinking?

JERRY

I'm sorry. *(to FAITH) No soy yo mismo.* I know what it's like to have... difficult... contrary...relatives.

CANDY

I'm sorry, too. I thought you guys were joking, that you were just trying to trigger each other. Playfully. My bad.

PAUL

Faith, I absolutely agree with you. This is your house and I...well...I got carried away. *(bows toward JERRY)* How can I make it up to you?

JERRY

(after a moment's reflection)
Sing. You're singers, right?
So, let's hear something.
Sing something pretty.

FAITH

"Carrickfergus". *(She
struggles to find it among
the sheet music.)* Our finest
hour.

JERRY

Yes!! That song rips my
heart out every time I hear
it. My mother was Irish. But
don't you need instruments?

MATTHEW

*(imitating the bandit in The
Treasure of the Sierra
Madre)* Instruments?
Instruments? We don't need
no stinking instruments.
*(PAUL and JERRY laugh.
CANDY does not.)*

CANDY

Another impossibly crude
Hispanic slur.

MATTHEW

No, it's something that...//

FAITH

Something stupid you used
to say as kids. But
something you should stop
saying now because you're
not kids anymore. At least
not actuarially.

CANDY

It's true, Matthew. You can't
use funny accents anymore.
Not around people who
through no fault of their
own were born with funny
accents. It's offensive.

MATTHEW

(to CANDY) I can't tell if
you're putting me on or not.

CANDY

I know. *(She giggles)*

PAUL

*(reassuring FAITH, who can't
find the music)* We'll do it
from memory. One verse.

MATTHEW

Remember to hum and
moan heavily. Act like the
Black and Tans just blew
through town. People will
think you're singing Gaelic.

*(PAUL beckons
FAITH into
singing
"Carrickfergus.")*

FAITH

"I wish I was in
Carrickfergus,
Only for nights in
Ballygrand."

MATTHEW

"I would swim o'er the
deepest ocean,
The deepest ocean to be by
your side."
*(Jerry moans and covers his
mouth.)*

PAUL

"But the sea is wide, and I
cannot swim over; and
neither have I the wings to
fly;
I wish I had a handsome

boatman
To ferry me over, my love
and I."

*(JERRY cries
hysterically while
the others stare
at PAUL, stunned
by his sincere,
heartfelt
performance.
PAUL, now
conscious of
being watched,
coughs and dabs
his eyes.)*

FAITH

(to PAUL) Thank you. *(to
MATTHEW)* Thank you.
*(JERRY applauds warmly
and embraces first FAITH,
then MATTHEW, and, after
some hesitation, PAUL, who
quickly pulls away.)*

JERRY

What a beautiful song! *Que
linda!*

PAUL

That song is who we are,
Jerry. It's us and it's ours.

JERRY

But it's such a gorgeous
song, why can't it be for
everyone?

CANDY

If things are for everyone,
don't they end up being for
no one, *amigo*?

JERRY

Mala mia. My bad. That
harmony fooled me. *(to
CANDY)* Enjoy your meal.
Nobody cooks better than
Faith. *Hay que seguir en
armonia, coqueta. (FAITH
glares at PAUL.)*

PAUL

Now I feel terrible. Terrible.
Faith, can Jerry stay with us
for dinner?

FAITH

Absolutely. I'll get more *vino*.

PAUL

Wonderful. What kind of
host lets a neighbor die of
thirst?

JERRY

(to PAUL) Hasta siempre, Comandante. Now *that's* Irish hospitality, which is exactly what I would expect from a McCarthy.

PAUL

We certainly can't have you leaving here thinking that there's any bad blood between us. I didn't come here to stir up trouble with the neighbors. *(to FAITH)* Am I speaking out of turn? Do we have enough to go around?

CANDY

What was it you said to me before, Faith, that when you were growing up you always had strangers breaking into your house and eating your food? So, you had to improvise. *A falta de pan, buenas son tortas.*

JERRY

(He sips a drink.) Love that saying. *Me encanta.* Repeat it to Archer constantly. *(to FAITH)* Means: If you run

150

out of bread, you can still
enjoy the cake.

MATTHEW

I think that's the kind of
material that got Marie
Antoinette into trouble.

FAITH

Don't worry, we've got
enough bread and cake and
farro salad. But one thing
that's *not* on the menu is
arguing.

PAUL

Dios mio, no! Trust me, I
have no animus toward
Jerry. *(to JERRY)* In fact, your
demographic group is very
important right now. *My*
people take *your* people
very seriously as a voting
bloc.

MATTHEW

Gay Jewish Black neighbors
with Irish mothers? That's a
voting bloc?

FAITH

The only group Jerry
belongs to is generous, kind,
fabulous-looking men.

CANDY

Kind and generous, *de
acuerdo*. Beyond that, I will
not go.

JERRY

And, Faith, that's why you're
my best friend. Not just on
this block, but in the whole
neighborhood, perhaps the
entire planet. *(to PAUL)*
Point of order, though: Are
you trying to convert me to
your side?

CANDY

*Moro viejo nunca será buen
cristiano*. That is: A leopard
cannot change its spots. It
has been scientifically
proven. In rigorously
monitored laboratory
settings.

JERRY

You're high, girl. A person can't change? I met Archer handing out flyers for Reagan. Wait, is it okay to say *that* President's name? Yes, back in the day, I was a young, black, Log Cabin Republican. *Jovenes Negros por Reagan. Lo juro.*

PAUL

You certainly get around. But how did you fall in with these guys, people that have to be on the right side of every single ethnic group's grievances? If Ronnie — the Great Communicator — was for anything, he was there for the average American.

CANDY

Good point, Pablo. Quite excellent. And forcefully argued.

FAITH

Why don't you just put on a cheerleader uniform, Candy?

CANDY

I can't help it if part of Paul's
incredible attraction for me
is the power and passion of
his political strategy.

MATTHEW

Didn't register so highly
with Paul's first three wives,

PAUL

(ignoring) Hey, I'm still the
same person I always was,
whether it's with the three
wives or jetting over to
Monaco or hosting an
incredibly popular
television show. I'm not the
one who set up camp in this
pious, preachy, self-
involved, little Northern
Jersey micro-enclave and let
it put me out of touch with
my people. Not to mention
out of touch with the
average American.

MATTHEW

Then, maybe you better
leave before you get
contaminated by non-
Aryans and race traitors.

Scurry back to your white
supremacist stronghold
down in the Sunshine State.

CANDY

Just because our village
happens to be filled with
white people doesn't mean
that they're white
supremacists. When black
communities are filled with
nothing but black people, no
one accuses *them* of being
black supremacists.

MATTHEW

Now there's a new take on the subject.

JERRY

You know what, *Princesa*?
I'm going to let that one go.
The truth is, I'm only here
for the farro salad.

FAITH

Look, Jerry, how about if I fix
you some take-out, so that
way you can go home and
not have to gag on this side
dish of sibling
obnoxiousness.

JERRY

Perfect. But could you
include an extra serving for
Archer? Just the farro salad?
Not the side-dish.

MATTHEW

(fixated) So, let me get this
straight: My lack of empathy
for every toothless trailer
park meth-head eating fried
Oreos out at the East
Podunk county fair makes
me an elitist betraying his
people?

PAUL

Yes.

MATTHEW

Fine. I'm an elitist. Won't
deny it. I want the elite
plumber to fix my toilet, and
the elite pizza guy to make
my tomato pie, and the elite
nurse to draw my blood.
And I always did. Regardless
of what you say, I haven't
changed one bit.

CANDY

Elite pizza guys do not exist.
Do not overstate your case.

JERRY

Oh, Faith, you haven't told
her about *Talula's?*
Sourdough pizza: farm to
table. And lavender-flavored
beignets!

MATTHEW

(ignoring JERRY) One thing
we can agree on: There's
nothing elite about your guy.

CANDY

Incorrect. Winners are
automatically the elite.
Being elected President of
the United States is to be the
ultimate elitist. *Es una
realidad.* But our president
confuses the opposition
because he plays four-
dimensional chess. He is
super-*elite,* but he has
deliberately decided not to
be part of *your* elite. And
that is something you
cannot understand.

157

JERRY

Archer plays four-
dimensional chess. Online.
Can't get enough of it.

FAITH

What on earth does four-
dimensional chess have to
do with anything?

MATTHEW

Instead of one board, you
have four, and (*gesturing to
indicate*) you designate
coordinates and there can
be a unicorn piece that
moves like a bishop, but...//

JERRY

Perdonme, but I think that
was a rhetorical question,
Matthew.

CANDY

*Poor Señor Matteo
Sabelotodo*! Too bad for you
know-it-alls that you aren't
the elite anymore.

FAITH

All the McCarthys are know-
it-alls. You'll find out. Wait
until Thanksgiving. They tell

you the best way to do
things, yet they personally
never leave the couch.

PAUL

At least some of us know
who we are.

MATTHEW

And who am I, Paul? Am I
the guy you called back in
1996 when Mom was in
hospice and you wanted to
get her into Enron?//

FAITH

(fiercely) No, you're the guy
who's going to remember
that we have a guest. Who
came for a meal, not legacy
leftover brotherly feuds. So,
now we will eat. Candy, why
don't you help me in the
kitchen? I can take
advantage of all that hands-
on waitressing experience
you accumulated before you
became a consultant.

CANDY

(grandly) Dissent
exterminator.

159

PAUL

Platinum level.

FAITH

Jerry, would you mind bringing in three extra chairs? You know where they are. Meanwhile, Matthew and Paul will have that conversation they both promised to have.

(FAITH & CANDY head to the kitchen.)

CANDY

Your party isn't turning out exactly the way you wanted, is it?

FAITH

You know, Candy, I don't get you. Is that all they taught you down in that doctoral program in Miami: Just agree with every goddamn thing your boyfriend says?

CANDY

I'm interested in maintaining a healthy relationship. What am I

supposed to do? Your
husband runs at the mouth
too. He's a real *el parlanchín*,
a chatterbox.

FAITH

Feel free to smack Matthew
down too. You have my
blessing.

CANDY

Oh, I see, you want me to
tear down the *patriarchy*?
(laughs) Good luck with
that. Yeah, I'm still a
feminist, but in my own
way......//

FAITH

Oh, in what way are you a
feminist, Candelaria?
Enlighten me. Please.

CANDY

To be a true feminist, a
woman must stop
fearing men. They are not
the enemy.

FAITH

You think I fear those two
bozos? Honey, you need to
lighten up on that bourbon.

CANDY

You fear whatever they're
going to say next. You want
to control them, and you
want me to imitate you.
Well, forget it. Eliminating
all those tiresome man-
grudges puts me on the
same level as them. But by
doing things my way, *I*
control my life. Instead of
always having to punch up.

FAITH

Just between us *feministas*:
That sounds like complete
and utter bullshit to me.

CANDY

I could take that as an insult,
but I won't. Taking
everything everyone says as
an insult is a leftist thing.

FAITH

Leftist? Because I *do*
appreciate getting along
with other people? Because I
don't think our purpose on
this earth is to constantly
pick fights. People like me —
we cooperate. We go along
to get along. Especially the
first time we visit
somebody's home.

CANDY

Cooperating. That's code for
wanting me to act like you.
You sound like my mother.

FAITH

I'm going to take that as a
compliment. *Familismo* and
all that.

CANDY

You should appreciate my
being different from you.
That way you can say you
have friends who are
diverse — and not just Jerry.
But I'm not like anybody
else.

FAITH

What does any of that have
to do with cooperating?

CANDY

Self-interest. Rational
selfishness. All the people
calling for cooperation can't
figure out how to get things
on their own. Ever read
Darwin? Survival of the
fittest?

FAITH

Yes, I have read Darwin.
Because being a biology
teacher in a blue state and
not in some cracker,
creationist backwater, I had
to. *Descent of Man*? "Those
that cared least for their
comrades would perish in
greater numbers"? Yeah, I
always enjoyed reading that
bit to the dumb-ass
sophomores.

CANDY

It's all about survival of the
fittest.

FAITH

News flash: Survivors
cooperate. Always have.
Want to know why? Because
if you piss off the other
members of the tribe they'll
slit your throat in your
sleep. That's how life really
works.

CANDY

That's just your opinion.

FAITH

No, that's *biology*,
Candelaria. The first
molecule that could copy
itself had to *cooperate* with
some other substance to
form the very first proto-
cell. Until those two things
cooperated, it was all just
primordial stew.

CANDY

Again, that's cells, not
people.

FAITH

What the fuck do you think
people are, Candy? Stem
Cells, Bone Cells, Blood Cells,

Muscle Cells, Fat Cells, Skin
Cells, Nerve Cells.

CANDY

You left out cancer cells.

FAITH

Throw them in too. The
more the merrier. Because
it's cells all the way down,
chica. Cooperating cells. It's
biology, whether we're
dissent exterminators or
stay-at-home moms.
Survivors are people who
find a way to fit in together.

CANDY

And sing corny old songs in
harmony.

FAITH

And sing corny old songs in
harmony. Bingo! Give that
gal a plush toy! Harmony
was – no, is -- definitely a
win-win. It sounds good. It
feels good. It *is* good. That's
biology too, Candy.

CANDY

(beat) I'm so hungry that the
only biology I care about

right now is human digestion. Did you know pythons eat more than a quarter of their body weight at one sitting? Honest. *(FAITH does not react, and CANDY becomes exasperated.)* I'm trying to make conversation. Doesn't that score points in the liberal rulebook?

FAITH

No. Now, let me ask you a question: How do you know that I'm not poisoning you?

CANDY

Don't be ridiculous, Faith.

FAITH

Ridiculous? Think again. Remember, I'm *Italiana*: Vergaretti. We Italians are very capable of poisoning our unsuspecting guests. And, yes, that's a crude ethnic stereotype. But the fucking Borgias proved that it was true.

CANDY

Poisoned and arrested in the
same night? Just like Paul
promised: Fun, fun, fun.

*(Lights shift to
living room:
PAUL and
MATTHEW sit in
silence while
JERRY carries in
the chairs.)*

JERRY

Oops! Did I miss the sibling
sit-down summit? The
mano-a-mano tête-à-tête?

PAUL

No. Not yet. *(gesturing
toward kitchen)* Faith
expects us to talk. *(beat)*
About my next book.

MATTHEW

"Require" is more like it.
Demand. Decree…//

JERRY

Perhaps I can be of some
assistance?

PAUL

How so?

JERRY

When I was in Nicaragua, the Sandinistas sometimes called upon me to be a hostage negotiator. So did the Contras. Those experiences could conceivably prove helpful in this situation.

PAUL

I figured we'd get to the Sandanistas eventually.

JERRY

Matthew, Paul, when we are confronted by opposing realities, our first step must be towards the opposite polarity. *(Both look at him, befuddled.)*

MATTHEW

And our second step?

JERRY

Want to take it from here, Paul?

PAUL

Matty, I would've offered the book to you on my own had you asked. *(silence, during which MATTHEW looks away awkwardly)* Christ sakes, Matty. We're family. This is what families do. They support each other, protect each other.

JERRY

Your turn, Matthew.

MATTHEW

Okay, so, as the elder statesman of the family, you're saying that you want to be the one to lead the attack on Amazon? Because they're the ones laying siege to our tiny, embattled publishing house.

PAUL

My side has plans for Amazon. Trust me. *(draws a finger across his throat)*

JERRY

(pouring his own big glass of wine) Now, *that's* the Paul McCarthy we all know and love in *our* house. Take no prisoners, Pablo!! *No pasaron!!!*

CANDY

(She shouts from the kitchen) Pasaran. With an "a."

PAUL

Everybody says my next book is going to be super-huge because of the TV tie-in.

JERRY

Pay attention, Matthew. *Oportunidad.* Knocking right on the *puerta.*

PAUL

(now conciliatory) So, we're good? *(He extends his hand. JERRY takes MATTHEW'S hand and, overcoming considerable resistance, clasps it to PAUL'S.)*

171

JERRY

A caballo regalado, no se le miran los dientes. (They look confused.) Don't look a gift horse in the mouth, Matthew.

PAUL

(attempting an awkward group hug) At long last, we have a deal.

(FAITH and CANDY enter from the kitchen, the former burdened with several plates, the latter carrying the corkscrew.)

Ah, Matty's wine. *(He opens the bottle.)* We need it for a toast: The McCarthy brothers have a new publishing venture — my latest best-selling book. I did it, Faith. Kept my promise. Matty is back in the fold. The Prodigal Son returns.

MATTHEW

Back in the fold with your fascist anti-vaxxer pals? And the miracle-cure con-men that buy ads on your show? And the...//

FAITH

Matty...

PAUL

Here we go again. Though, by the sound of it, you *do* watch my show, don't you?

MATTHEW

Yes, but don't flatter yourself too much. I also watch YouTube videos of massively unsuccessful heart transplants.

FAITH

Matthew, what are you doing?

MATTHEW

He said we're back in the fold. So, I'm just getting a read on what you've gotten us into, *mi amor. (FAITH is now fuming.)*

PAUL

It's okay, Faith. The important thing is to get

your little publishing house on the best-seller's list. And now, on to this fabulous feast we've all been waiting for. And some more of this fabulous wine. *(He drinks up.)* From California.

JERRY

Sounds good to me. *(He takes a big swig.)* Faith, Matthew, would you mind if I invited Archer over? He positively adores *familismo*. And farro salad. And he'd love to meet Paul. *(He rises and moves to the side to make his call.)* Disculparme un momento.

MATTHEW

Yeah, invite Archer, Jerry. Let's get everybody into the fold.

FAITH

(suspicious) Of course, Jerry. We have plenty of food. *(eyeing MATTHEW)* And if people are eating, they're less likely to say foolish things.

CANDY

I agree. I'm starving. Is it
okay if we help ourselves?
*(FAITH does not yet pass the
platter.)*

JERRY

(into the phone) No, I didn't
get lost, Archer. Turned out I
got to do a little mediating
for Faith.

MATTHEW

Foolish things? Who here
would ever say foolish
things? You mean like
predicting concentration
camps for conservatives?
(beat) Exploring the non-
existent Kenya connection?
That sort of thing?

FAITH

For the love of Christ, not
Kenya again.

CANDY

(tipsy now) I would love to
go to Kenya. It's supposed to
be very beautiful. With
many, many wildebeests.
And cheetahs.

JERRY

(covering phone) Not that
many wildebeests. That's
more over in Botswanaland.
Lots of zebras, though. *(back
on phone)* Archer, either
turn down the Puccini or
turn up your hearing aid!

PAUL

What? You never said
something offensive, little
brother? Never?

MATTHEW

That's the point, Paul. I
know every time I've fucked
up. But racist propaganda
never...//

FAITH

Every time? Does this count
as one of those fuck-ups, *mi
amor? (She moves bottle
away to the sideboard.)*
Forget it. Let's change the
topic.

CANDY

What was that part about
Kenya?

FAITH

Oh, it was probably before
you met...

CANDY

Were you a birther, Paul?
(She laughs hysterically.) Oh,
my God, you were kidding,
right? You were just trolling
him. *(to Matthew)* I think
you're upset because he
kind of owns you, Matty.

MATTHEW

Oh, he owns me, does he,
Dulcinea?

FAITH

Easy there. Let's take things
down a few notches.

JERRY

(covering phone again)
Please say that you're not a
birther, Paul. It would break
Archer's heart if you were.
His *corazon* would be...
muerta.

CANDY

Muerto. Masculine. And the
word you are looking for is
roto. But everybody knows

177

that all that birth certificate
stuff was just a way of
triggering liberals? Just
something our side dreamed
up for laughs? *(She giggles
at MATTHEW, but JERRY,
insulted, stares and again
picks up the phone.)*

MATTHEW

Ah, so being a racist *is* part
of being in the fold?

CANDY

Racist? Now we *know* we're
behind socialist lines, Papi.

JERRY

(into the phone) Get over
here; yes, it's *that* Paul
McCarthy.

PAUL

Always playing the race
card. Mom never told you,
Matty, but you were born
white. *(singing)* Born White!
*(laughs at his own joke and
drains his glass)* And guess
what? It's nothing to be
ashamed of, either.

CANDY

Besides, isn't everyone
naturally biased to some
extent, Matty? Isn't that
simple *biology*, Faith?

MATTHEW

Candelaria, you're not
family, so please don't call
me Matty.

PAUL

Don't start with Candy,
Matty. Bad idea.

FAITH

Both of you, stop. Final
warning.

JERRY

(*into phone*) I'm sure he
would autograph it. Yes, free
of charge.

MATTHEW

Hey, hey, hey. I thought we
could talk about anything in
this daring new age. Not so?

PAUL

Sure, let's do that, Matty. But
do you really want to bring

up racism in front of Jerry,
given the racist things that
came out of your mouth
over the years. Just to show
us all how funny you were.

CANDY

Oh, I want to hear this!
Digame, Pablito! Digame!

MATTHEW

Me saying racist things?

PAUL

Well, the n-word.

MATTHEW

(livid) What the hell does
that mean?

PAUL

You said that word. *(He
stands and follows
MATTHEW.)* Lots of times.
Don't deny it.

JERRY

(into phone) No. Do not wear
that vest. Do not.

MATTHEW

Never.

PAUL

You sang it. *(singing)* *"Boom, boom, boom, boom."*

FAITH

What are you talking about?

PAUL

(singing) Two little...

MATTHEW

Don't you dare!

JERRY

(On the phone) I don't know what we're having for dessert. *(eying MATTHEW)* Hang on. Might have to work in a bit of conflict resolution here.

PAUL

Are you ashamed? Oh yes, let's sing that classic. *(singing) "Boom, boom, boom, boom! I see your heinie. Boom, boom, boom, boom! So black and shiny. Boom, boom, boom, boom! But when it wiggles..."* *(speaking)* But that's not how it starts, is it? Can you remember the beginning?

Because we *all* sang that
song.

MATTHEW

Singing a silly song as a kid
is not the same thing as
race-baiting along with the
Con-man-in-Chief...

PAUL

But you admit that you sang
it. In fact, looking back on
things, that might have been
the start of our singing
career. *(singing)* "*Boom,
boom, boom, boom...*"

FAITH

It's not funny, Paul. Don't ...
don't...

PAUL

(over her) "*Two little ni...*"

MATTHEW

(shouting over PAUL) No!

FAITH

I said don't!

*(Matthew bull-rushes Paul,
but Jerry jumps in throwing
both to the floor. Paul rises*

*up, only to collapse with
another 'attack.' Matthew,
on his knees, holds his back
in pain. Candy hurries to
Paul, who rolls away. She
sniffs the air before tending
to him. Faith stares down at
Matthew while Jerry stands
guard.)*

FAITH

No. *(progressively louder)*
No! *(PAUL recovers after the
gas attack, gestures.)* No!
(MATTHEW starts to speak.)
No! *(CANDY gives her a
look.)* And in Spanish? *No,
nunca.* A good time was had
by all? *(She solicits their
confirmation.)* Bueno. Now
get out. Get out. All of you.
Pronto.

CANDY

Why? What did I do?

FAITH

What did you do? Nothing. I
know all about doing
nothing. In fact, maybe I'll
write a book for our do-
nothing publishing house
called *What I Did for the
Fucking McCarthys.* A
cliffhanger where the

heroine goes missing for
thirty years.

PAUL

Hey, hey, hey! You're
blaming me? But I did
exactly what you wanted.
Gave you the book. Saved
the publishing house. And I
never said either of the
names...

FAITH

You mean "Trump?" Is that
it? Trump? (*yelling*) Trump?
(*beat*) Was that the
forbidden name? No, you
didn't say *it*. Now I did.
Deliberately. Trump. Trump.
Trump. Trump. Trump. (*in
CANDY'S face*) Oh-Bomb-Ah!
Oh-Bomb-Ah! And just for
good measure, let me throw
in Hillary. Hillary. Hillary.
Hillary. I'm not even sure
how much any of this
matters to... this. They're
just the latest excuses for
you two to argue, to see
who's smarter, who can sing
the higher note, who can be
so right and never wrong.

Well, I am no longer amazed
or even amused. I hate the
fact that I ever was.

PAUL

I apologize. I do. How about
this? We'll have dinner in
silence. Or no, we'll stay and
we'll sing. *(half-singing)* So
sorry, dear Faith. So sorry.
*(He stops, as she is visibly
unmoved.)* And to you too,
Jerry.

JERRY

*Llamando a la puerta
equivocada. (PAUL is
puzzled.)*

CANDY

(translating) You're barking
up the wrong tree.

MATTHEW

Yeah, we'll sing and make
up.

CANDY

Different songs, though. *Por
favor.*

FAITH

Sing? Sing? Sorry, the hootenanny is over. And by the way, Paul, you think you know how my father would have voted? I don't even know, but I do know what he would have said tonight after listening to you two. *Mi fa cagare*! Need a translation, *carino*? "It makes me shit."

PAUL

Faith, I *am* terribly sorry. I just wanted to help. But Matty pushes my...//

MATTHEW

Hang on a second...

FAITH

You don't have a say in this, *o sole mio. (to Paul)* Neither of you do. *(sing-song, like PAUL)* Good-bye. Good-bye. Good-bye.

CANDY

Faith, Paul is still Matty's brother.

MATTHEW

Don't call me Matty.

FAITH

Well, he's not my brother.
So, he can get out. Forever.
And Candelaria, on your way
out, keep your goddamn
hands off other people's
signs, because this time I
won't stop the cops from
locking up your hot little
libertarian ass.

MATTHEW

Faith, this dinner was your
idea.

FAITH

This? *(She swings her arms
to indicate the entire scene,
then flings a plate of
breadsticks into the air.)* No!
This (pause) was not my
idea! My idea was to get the
old trio together for *one*
festive and joyous night of
singing. That's all I wanted.
Well, we're not a trio
anymore. Once upon a time
never comes again.

MATTHEW

But, Faith...

FAITH

You got a problem? Then go
with him. Good riddance.
*(MATTHEW hesitates. He is
not leaving.)* No? I didn't
think so, *Tesoro.* Jerry, you
stay. And get Archer over
here.

JERRY

*(bowing) Seria un placer, mi
reina.*

CANDY

Look, people, it's late. And
I'm starving. And you've
slaved over this wonderful
dinner all evening. And the
cauliflower is getting cold.
(*to FAITH*) So, what are we
supposed to eat?

FAITH

Me no know. Go ask Pepe.

JERRY

Uh-oh...

CANDY

I can't believe you're saying
that...

FAITH

Oh, yes you can. Of course,
you can. Because there's
nothing beyond belief
anymore. Nothing. That's
the truth. *Es la realidad.*

(*FAITH grabs the
Farro salad
platter, swinging
it just out of
CANDY'S reach.
Cradling it, she
picks up a piece
of prosciutto and
eats it
lingeringly,
sensually. The
others stand
immobile. The
lights dim as she
backs into the
kitchen, singing.*)

FAITH

*Vayan con Dios, muchachos.
Vaya con dios*, my love.

END OF PLAY

Milton Keynes UK
Ingram Content Group UK Ltd.
UKHW050223130724
445574UK00013B/635